SHADOW
SIGHT

ALSO BY T. G. AYER

Young Adult Paranormal

THE VALKYRIE SERIES

Dead Radiance

Dead Radiance Audio

Dead Embers

Dead Embers Audio

Dead Chaos

Dead Chaos Audio

Dead Wrath

Dead Silence

Joshua - Dead Radiance

Joshua II - Dead Embers

Joshua III - Dead Chaos

Joshua IV - Dead Wrath

Joshua V - Dead Silence

THE HAND OF KALI SERIES

Fire & Shadow

Blood & Gold

Time & Fate

Fury & Virtue

Spirit & Soul

∾

Adult Sci-Fi

HANDS ASSASSIN

Death Dealer
Death Mark
Death Strike
Hand's Assassins Series

∾

NEW ADULT CONTEMPORARY THRILLER W/A TONI VALLAN

Beautiful Collision
Beautiful Conviction

∾

PSYCHOLOGICAL HORROR W/A TONI VALLAN

Dark Shadows
Splinter

SHADOW SIGHT

A DARK SIGHT NOVEL #3

Cover art by Eduardo Priego

Cover art © T.G. Ayer. All rights reserved.

ISBN-13: 978-0995112629

ISBN-10: 0995112622

INFINITE INK BOOKS

SHADOW SIGHT

USA TODAY BESTSELLING AUTHOR
T.G. AYER

AUTHOR'S NOTE

Thank you for reading my Dark Sight Series. Shadow Sight is the close of our story arc with Langcourt. Throughout the story, we learn a lot about the Pythias of the past and the horrors they faced. As such, I wanted to be sure and provide my readers with a possible trigger warning. The story includes brief descriptions of past domestic violence and the toll it took on the Pythia who was abused.

Thank you so much for joining me on this journey into Allegra's world. It has been amazing, researching and playing around with alternative endings to our world's history.

The Dark Sight world has fascinated me through my writing journey, so much so, that I still remain inspired with many more ideas brewing within this universe.

T.G. Ayer

CHAPTER 1

*W*ater. What had once given Allegra Damascus a sense of peace and safety, was now about to kill her.

Until recently, Allegra had sought a sense of tranquility, a semblance of serenity in immersing herself in water whether it be the pool at her home in the Venara Hills in Fornia, or in the waters of the Endless Sea along the Fornia coast.

Of course, that was only until the god Neptune had attempted to kill her.

Memories of that awful night returned, flooding her mind and Allegra was again trapped within the dark waters of the Endless Sea, waves surging around her as some inexplicable force pulled her deeper and deeper into blackest depths of the ocean.

And now, again, Allegra was trapped beneath the waves, so far beneath the surface that had she been able to see out into the ocean's depths, she knew she'd have no sight of anything, least of all the surface.

Thankfully, her black pants and skintight sweater hadn't made things any worse for her. But her military-issue boots had weighed her down, the laces grown so thick, engorged with water, that all her attempts at opening them had failed. She'd resorted to slicing through the ties with her bejeweled dagger, though she'd winced at the time, wondering what Aurelia would have thought of such a menial use for the beautiful weapon.

Allegra blinked, then moved her hand to brush the hair floating around her head out of her eyes. Her long dark blonde locks trailed around her face, like strands of seaweed attempting to engulf her, to suffocate her.

She was trapped in a cabin, aboard the *Lady Makara*, a ship that had turned out to be a pirate vessel. Allegra was not surprised that the rickety, rust-bucket had ended up blowing an engine, taking on water, and slowly sinking to the seabed. The explosion had been an accident waiting to happen, and more perhaps a curse upon the traffickers who'd lured good, hard-working people into their filthy traps with lies and promises of a better life.

Allegra was glad she wasn't a god, because she would not have hesitated in striking the men responsible down with a single flick of a finger.

With her lungs pulsing, screaming for air, and her body convulsing, Allegra shook her head, unable to hold out even a second longer. She pushed upward, using the corner of the captain's desk to kick off hard, and her body moved through the shadowed water, floating upward until she reached the roof of the cabin. The sinking *Lady Makara*, which had tilted at a slight angle as it drifted to the seabed, had serendipitously provided Allegra with her only means with which to stay breathing and alive. Caught in the corner of the cabin was a precious pocket of air which Allegra was currently using as sparingly as possible, biding her time in the hopes that someone would come for her.

That someone was more than likely going to be Max.

As much as Allegra had to admit she dreaded seeing him again, she had to also accept that there was no other man she'd want to be the one to pluck her from the depths and wrap his arms around her.

"Snap out of it, Allegra," she muttered silently. "You're showing sure signs of delirium."

Max Vissarion was going to be furious with her. Echoing in Allegra's mind was Max's voice as he'd demanded she remain at home on Aurelia's estate in the Charrúa Ranges of Argentina, as he'd insisted her presence was not required to facilitate the rescue of the refugees.

"It's not necessary for you to accompany us, Allegra," Max had insisted, his dark eyes flashing as he'd attempted to reason with her. "Surely you see that I'm not being unreasonable. Your life is worth a hundred of ours. Let us go and save those people. Your vision was clear enough for us to know the dangers they faced, clear enough that we can avert the disaster."

Max's face had darkened with anger and frustration, and he'd let out a frustrated groan when Allegra had merely shaken her head in response before saying, "I'm coming, Max. Don't try to stop me."

Now, Allegra let out a relieved sigh as she broke the surface and expelled a long-stale breath. She craned her neck and lifted her face clear of the water. Taking a few deep breaths, Allegra sank again—fueled again by re-oxygenation and renewed hope— then swam toward the door to the cabin.

Allegra grabbed the handle and tugged as hard as she could, blinking as her movements made her hair float forward around her face, the strands fanning out and teasing her face and eyes. She shook the hair away and pulled again, eyes bugging as she tugged with the desperation of someone who knows that death is imminent.

In most cases, Allegra herself would have been the one to insist they keep going, to demand they not stop until they'd reached their goal, saved the people she'd seen dying horrible deaths in some disaster or tragedy. But today, she was all out of pep talks, all out of passion and determination.

Another tug, and then another—Allegra strained hard, ignoring the stabbing in her lungs as she put all her strength behind the force of her pull. But the door still wouldn't budge. She let out a groan that burst from her lips in a flotilla of bubbles that drifted and swirled all the way to the ceiling.

Allegra slammed a fist against the cabin door and pushed off again, surging up to the ceiling. She broke through the surface and then gulped in the air, taking deep breaths as she forced herself to calm down. She was about to take her final breath when everything around her shuddered, a low groan reverberating within the cabin. The ship tilted to the side a little more, and then with another growling shudder, it began to slide. Panic engulfed Allegra as she kicked hard to get to the air pocket again, to grab one last breath before she lost her chance altogether.

The ship shook violently now, tilting further on its side. And then the pocket of air was gone.

Allegra let out a muffled cry and floated away, her back thudding softly against the bulkhead. She closed her eyes and thought about the people she and Max and Athena had saved. She'd done her duty. Wasn't that all that really mattered?

It wouldn't matter if she died. As long as all those innocent people were safe.

CHAPTER 2

*T*en days ago, Allegra had awakened from a terrible dream, filled with horror and panic.

Her skin was slick with sweat, and she twisted urgently, her body still within the dream's clutches. She surged from the bed so fast that her feet caught and tangled within the bedsheets. She lost her balance and tipped over the side of the bed.

The moonlight lit the stone tiles, and Allegra found it incongruous to be able to see the floor flying at her face. She'd have hit the floor face first, if not for the firm, warm grip around her ankle.

Max.

He grunted, his fingers tightening around her foot. "I got you," he murmured, reaching for her with his other hand.

Max grasped her around her waist and gathered her to him, pulling her back onto the mattress and laying her gently alongside him.

"Are you all right?" he asked softly, studying her face in the shadowed light of the moon.

Allegra nodded, turned toward him, seeking his warmth. "I'm

fine. Thanks for saving my ass," she whispered resting her cheek against his chest.

Max chuckled, then reached behind her and slapped her ass. "Don't think it needed saving. Was the face that was heading for a smashing," he said, though behind the laughter lay a hint of worry.

Allegra grimaced. "I really thought I was going to hit the floor." Then she smiled up at Max. "How fortuitous that our decision to 'shack up together' had come just in time."

Despite the banter, Allegra found she couldn't shake off the memory of her vision; the faces of the dead from the dream now haunted her waking moments.

And it must have shown on her face.

Max placed a finger on her chin and tilted her face toward him. "Tell me," he said softly, concern in his eyes even though he tried to hide it.

Allegra swallowed then took a deep breath, extracting herself from his arms. She lay back on her pillow and stared up at the ceiling. "Children, whole families, all crammed inside the hold of a ship...and it sinks and kills them all." She shook her head, unable to stop feeling as though she was right there with them even now.

Max rubbed her arm gently, his touch more comforting than he even knew. "Can you think of anything?" he asked gently, now doing his job. "Any details you can recall?"

Allegra shifted from the bed and got to her feet, pacing the moonlit floor as she gave Max the details, her skin cold from the memory of drowning in the bottom of that ship.

Max had moved fast, retrieving his ever-present notebook and pen before guiding Allegra through the vision and finessing details from her that she hadn't thought to consider.

"Can you see any signs or written warnings?"

Allegra nodded, then hurried to the box beneath the window. She lifted the lid and retrieved a parchment and a pen, needing to feel the movement to invoke a more detailed memory. She laid the paper on the floor and began to scribble what she'd seen in the vision.

It turned out, after Max had done his part of the investigation, that Allegra had written out words in the Mon script of the Mranma people.

Words that had spelled out the name of a small charter vessel, the *Lady Makara*. The same ship that had sunk only minutes before.

Taking Allegra with it to the bottom of the seabed.

CHAPTER 3

*M*ax let out a growl of frustration as he glared at the Oracle of Delphi, the flickering torchlight from the bow revealing her stiff spine and taut neck as she stalked toward the port-side ladder of the *Royal Yakshi*.

In the darkness, the rest of her body—encased in a dark sweater and pants, and heavy boots—blended into the shadows.

They'd arrived in Kan Taung Gyi, a small town along the coast of Mranma and had boarded the *Yakshi* from a small inlet a mile south. They'd reached the refugee ship with barely a moment to spare as it had already begun to sink into the dark depths of the river.

Allegra had cited an explosion in the engine room as the cause, a result of a number of successive visions which she'd begun to refer to as blinks.

Now, Max held his tongue even when the Pythia began to descend the ladder, her golden head disappearing from view as she made her way to the waiting boats.

"Did you really think you were going to win that argument?" asked Athena, a smirk curving her lips, her eyes glittering with amusement. The demigod moved her dark braid aside then tossed her mission kit-bag over her shoulder and lifted an eyebrow, clearly waiting for him to reply.

Max grunted again, suspecting the demigod's loyalty lay with Allegra first. "Perhaps I had harbored some meager hope that she would listen to reason?" he muttered, reaching for his own bag of supplies.

The team had suited up, all wearing black pants, beanies and sweaters, military issue boots and a selection of belts and straps to house their knives and guns.

Athena snorted as she paused at the hatch to swing herself around. "I was under the impression you knew her well," she said as she placed a foot on the first rung of the ladder.

Max flicked a glance at Allegra who now sat in the first boat, facing the sinking *Lady Makara* a few hundred meters across the water. "Are you in support of her rashness?" Max bit the question out, still staring at Allegra, then turned his attention and raised an eyebrow at Athena as she paused mid-step and looked up at him.

"I am waiting to make a decision," she replied serenely. "Right now, I see a woman who is strong-minded, powerful, intelligent, and determined. She knows her purpose, and she wants to make her mark. Do you really want to be the one to kill her spirit?"

Max snorted. "I suppose that point would be rather moot if she succeeds in getting herself killed," he muttered. Athena's eyes widened, and Max knew he'd hit his mark.

Yet, the demigod did not pause to agree with him. Instead, she descended the ladder, her head held just as regally as her mistress the Pythia. Max waited until Athena had descended and joined Allegra in the first of the small flotilla. From the last rung, he jumped into the waiting boat and nodded at the sailor to move out, to lead the way to the sinking ship.

Captain Alrait of the *Royal Yakshi* had sent out a team of divers to scan the vessel and advise on the best way to access the hold and rescue the people Allegra had seen in her vision. The only problem was, the oracle had seen the vision all too correctly. Max and the team had arrived to find the captain of the *Lady Makara* and his crew had fled. Max wasn't happy that he'd been unable to at least sight the criminals, but he did have the boat's registration details, and he planned on tracking the lowlifes down as soon as they'd retrieved the refugees.

When the dive team returned, they confirmed the explosion had originated in the engine room; their only access point to the hold was the bow deck entrance which thankfully was still above water.

Allegra had been so angry and had received one of her blinks. A brief vision, but enough to confirm that there were still people on board the sinking ship and that nothing had changed from what she'd seen in her initial vision—those people were still going to die if Max and their team didn't do something about it.

Filled with both fear and anger, Allegra had demanded she join them on the rescue mission, insisting that they needed every pair of hands they could get. She'd had a point—Alrait's men had appeared reluctant to help, and Max wasn't sure they'd go out of their way to save those people.

In the face of Allegra's demands, Max had known then and there that, other than tying the woman up and tossing her into the captain's cabin, he had little choice but to allow her to go. Even her promise that she'd be careful had rung hollow for Max.

It was his stupid gut, some strange feeling he'd had the moment Allegra had told him of that vision. He'd been tempted to tell her he'd been unable to identify the words she'd drawn out for him—which had turned out to be the name of the slave ship now sinking into the River Dalet. But he'd thought better. Allegra, despite her sweet nature, was not the sort of person a man would be okay with crossing.

The three rowboats reached the sinking vessel, which by now was half-submerged, though the deck remained at a shallow incline, still above the water.

"Appears to be listing to one side," said Max, his voice carrying over the water to the boat beside him where Allegra and Athena both stared at the sinking vessel. "There's a good chance whoever is trapped inside is still alive. If the hold were flooded, the ship would have disappeared into the water by now."

"Let's hope you're right," said Allegra softly.

Max didn't reply. He waited for his rowboat to slow as it reached the rungs that lead up to the bow deck and ascended it, aware that Allegra was not far behind him.

On deck, Max proceeded to yell orders to Captain Alrait and his men, then watched as they dispersed to search the ship. They returned within minutes to report the discovery of the families hidden in the hold. The refugees were a sad sight; three families of five or six, the parents much older than Max had expected. Either that, or the adults were young, but a hard life had run them down.

Max called out, directing the relieved refugees toward the three boats. Allegra had been on the deck, guiding the women and children down to the crafts, and when they'd confirmed everyone was on the boats, Max had instructed them to return to the *Yakshi*.

That had been the last he'd seen of Allegra.

"WHAT DO you mean you have no idea where she is?" Max yelled at Athena, caring little that the woman could shift into a deadly jaguar and rip his throat out before he blinked again.

"She was just behind me," Athena said firmly, glancing over her shoulder and pointing at one of the three men they'd saved. "The man over there...he said he told Allegra that his daughter and another young girl had been taken away from the families the moment they'd boarded. The captain had said the girls would be safe in his cabin, but the two fathers hadn't been convinced. Hence the black eyes and bruises."

"So Allegra went back to find the girls?" Max asked through gritted teeth.

In unison, Max and Athena turned and looked over at the sinking *Lady Makara*. At the same moment, the sound of screaming rent the air and Max spotted two small girls on the bow of the now almost fully-submerged ship, waving madly and screaming at the top of their voices.

"She found them," yelled Athena as she raced for the ladder with Max close on her heels.

But retrieving the two terrified girls had only heightened Max's fear for Allegra, a fear made worse as the ship disappeared beneath the waves with a hollow gurgle.

Panic ensued in the next few minutes as Max called for divers, as three sailors stripped and dove deep inside the murky waters. More sailors hung over the edge of their boat, holding torchlights above the water in the hopes to aid the divers in their search and lighting their way.

Minutes passed with Max diving, again and again, hoping each time that he'd see Allegra. The interior of the ship had been thoroughly flooded, half in pieces, the other bent out of shape. Max had swum the corridors toward the captain's cabin to find it barred. The two girls had been scared out of their minds but had insisted that the golden lady had left the ship with them.

Max returned to the boats and counted the minutes, each passing once making him feel more and more angry and sick to his stomach.

"Xales will find her, Max," Athena had said, attempting to make him feel better. But her words served to only fuel his anger because this was proof that he'd been right to worry about Allegra.

"It's way past five minutes, Athena. Xales may have to work a miracle for her this time," Max whispered as he stared out at the dark waters, holding back his terror as he watched every wave, every glint of moonlight on the sea, praying that the next flash of movement would prove to be Allegra, resurfacing, proving his fears wrong.

But he saw nothing.

CHAPTER 4

*A*llegra blinked as the cabin shifted again. Something was happening, the vessel was turning around as it sank ever deeper. From looking at the *Lady Makara* when they'd arrived, Allegra would never have thought the inlets and channels wending their way through the islands along the Dalet River would have gone so deep.

Spurred by panic, Allegra grabbed hold of the door handle and only waited until the tumbling ship had done a half roll, bringing her to stand upright for the briefest second.

Allegra pulled the handle hard, putting all her strength behind it. And the door opened, swinging in so suddenly that had Allegra not been floating in the water, she would likely have fallen on her ass.

Now, though, she pulled herself toward the threshold and swam into the corridor. Her chest tightened, and she thought about that precious air pocket that was lost to her just when she'd needed it the most. With all the spinning the ship had done, that air pocket would have been shifted around the room, or it could have been sucked away entirely.

Forcing herself to think of getting to safety now that she'd been freed from the cabin, Allegra swam hard, making her way down the corridor, well aware that she'd long passed the time when she'd needed to take another breath in order to remain alive.

Up ahead was the main corridor that led to the exterior door to the deck. With freedom and safety in sight, Allegra now pushed herself to the limit. She took the corner at the fastest speed she was capable of while submerged.

And slammed straight into the man who'd locked the girls inside that cabin in the first place.

The captain.

He floated in the corridor, eyes wide open, a long piece of metal impaling him through the heart. The water around him was a red-brown, his blood seeping out of his body and tainting the space around him.

The shock of seeing him was enough that Allegra let out a low scream and backpedaled, too late realizing she had no way to take another breath. So much of the oxygen in her lungs had been depleted, and she was now left with barely anything to help her while she made the rest of the way to the surface.

Still, Allegra blinked hard, gave the dead man a wide berth and swam for the door. Pushing it open, she felt a surge of relief that she was free. Above her, the light of the moon—along with a handful of torches—lit the surface, and despite how far away it appeared, Allegra could almost taste her freedom.

Her lungs screamed, but she ignored them, willed them to understand the pressure she was putting them under. *Just hold on. Only a moment or two more.*

Swimming hard, Allegra didn't see the broken chimney tilting toward her—at least not until it cast a dark shadow over her. And by then it was already too late.

The solid metal hit her broadside, slammed the rest of the air from her lungs and drew a blanket of blackness over her.

ALLEGRA OPENED HER EYES, blinking against the pain in her head and back. But as awareness returned, she registered the absence of that pain. And the absence of water altogether.

Eyes widening, Allegra stared around her, sucking in a shocked breath. She stood in a room, tiled floor to ceiling in white. Dark paintings—undulating spirals and swirling geometric shapes in deep rich plum and moss, indigo, and bronze —dotted the walls, lending the space an elegant feel.

But despite the decor, the room appeared sterile, with only a picture window that revealed rough, roiling waves as they crashed against a rocky shoreline, spray surging high to create a cloud of mist.

A single white bed occupied the center of the room, its shape curving gently to fit the form of its occupant, making it appear more like a recliner than a mattress.

Allegra watched the woman; she lay there, golden hair splayed along the white pillow like liquid as she stared out of the window, Allegra hesitated, then felt her body shift forward, as though she was not in control of her limbs.

The woman moved her attention from the picture window to Allegra, her eyes widening, filled with relief and sadness.

"You came," she whispered, her voice still echoing around the sterile room. "I was afraid you wouldn't hear me."

Allegra found herself answering, "I heard you, my child. I just needed a little assistance in getting here."

Allegra stiffened. *What is going on here?*

The woman on the bed let out a mirthless chuckle. "Not something we are used to, is it?"

Allegra heard the voice reply, "The Pythian line is made of much sterner stuff. Prevailing is in our DNA." The voice, though it did appear to have come from Allegra, wasn't hers at all. In fact, Allegra felt as though she was somehow overlaid upon the

17

speaker, performing her actions though unable to access her thoughts.

The golden-haired woman's face darkened and her amusement faded. "I'm afraid in this instance, Mother Aurelia, we may not prevail. Not unless we do something…fast."

Aurelia?

Allegra's blood ran cold. Aurelia? Had Allegra somehow traveled to a place where Aurelia had been in her past? The room looked unusual, far more technologically advance than one would expect for Aurelia's lifetime, though Allegra wasn't arrogant enough to assume she knew everything of what her predecessor would have seen in her days as the Pythia.

Besides, Aurelia as the speaker did make sense, that voice was familiar enough from Allegra's own dream-visions. Though confused, Allegra was far too curious to attempt to pull free from this particular dream-trance.

She stepped closer and stopped beside the bed, observing as she—or rather, Aurelia—reached for the woman's hands. "Jocasta, my child. What is it you need help with? Apollo was clear when he sent me. You need help that you cannot get in this future time?" said Aurelia.

Allegra startled, staring around her again, taking in the technologically advanced equipment, monitoring screens embedded within the walls, fiber optics shimmering on the surface of the bed, probably monitoring Jocasta's condition.

Something about the woman pulled on Allegra, a certain familiarity, as though they'd met somewhere before. But Allegra forced herself to focus on Aurelia's words as the Pythia leaned closer to Jocasta and squeezed her hands.

"It's the baby," Jocasta said, tears glistening in her eyes. "I know I was supposed to…I know I came to do something important, to keep the line of the Pythia alive. But there is…you need to know…I have not failed you because I wasn't taking my role seriously. Mother would not have been very happy with me. And it's likely even that she can still see me."

Allegra leaned toward Jocasta as Aurelia said, "Child, you are rambling and time is of the essence. I do not know how much time I have as this is the first time that I have used this particular spell. So it is best we not waste time, dear girl."

Jocasta drew a deep shuddering breath. "I apologize, Mother Aurelia." She stared out the window for a brief moment. "I'm not going to be around to bring her up, to show her what being a Pythia is all about."

Aurelia took the last step toward the bed that brought her close enough to hold Jocasta in her arms. She curled her arm around the distraught woman's shoulders, and as she did so, Allegra felt a rippling against her own skin, an awareness that she couldn't define, couldn't explain.

"Please, child," whispered Aurelia, "I know it is difficult, but you must tell me what I came to hear. There is a good chance I may be pulled out of this joining at any moment."

Jocasta sniffed and wiped her nose with the back of her hand. "I have leukemia. Cancer of the blood. I will not survive the child's first year of life. Despite the technology of this time, there is little they can do to stop the disease as it was discovered in early pregnancy and termination would have been the only way that I could have received the treatment."

"And you refused the treatment?"

Jocasta nodded.

"Why would you do that?" asked Aurelia, and Allegra felt her confusion, understood it too.

"To protect the Pythian line," Jocasta said, her eyes beseeching and yet filled with regret. "I have seen the devastation to our kind, I've watched so many wonderful women be slaughtered. I could not sit back and allow that awful man to take one more of our sisters."

"*He* did this to you?" asked Aurelia, probably as horrified as

Allegra was at the prospect that Langcourt had the power to give a Pythia a deadly disease.

Jocasta shook her head. "No. Not that I know of. I just meant that he was the reason I was sent to this time. We were all sent away to protect us. So many different places, all of us separated from those we loved most in the world."

Jocasta was rambling again, but Allegra noticed that Aurelia didn't urge her to hurry.

"I was so afraid when I found out about cancer," Jocasta said, her eyes shimmering with tears as she looked away, out of the window as though some form of solace lay within the view. "My husband, he insisted that I take the treatment, said we could try again afterward. But the doctor confirmed that after this child, I would not be able to have any more." She let out a soft, pained laugh and looked back at Aurelia. "That was it for me. I could not see a future in which I killed a Pythia. What if *she* is the last living Pythia of our line? And I would kill her? No. Not a chance."

Aurelia patted Jocasta's shoulder. "I wish I could have been here to help you through this. Perhaps we could have found a different way."

"There isn't," Jocasta said vehemently, shaking her head, eyes wide and pleading again as though she thought Aurelia was already thinking of alternatives. "The doctors have confirmed I have no more than a month left now. There will be transfusions, radiation therapy."

"May I ask why the treatment won't work?"

"Honestly?" Jocasta asked. Then she let out a laugh, the ragged sound laced with bitter irony. "It actually might work. But I cannot risk taking the treatment. It would mean they will test my blood."

"Which is a good thing, perhaps?" said Aurelia gently.

Aurelia may not have understood where Jocasta was leading, but Allegra did. Research and testing on a person with powers.

Jocasta shook her head. "Not! It is not a good thing at all.

Once they test my blood, they will see I've not been immunized at the correct times for this time period. That I have not been treated for the H7T4 that was rampant when I arrived here twenty years ago. Mother sent me here just after a devastating flu struck the world. It reduced the population by forty percent, and the remaining survivors were injected with antibodies. Nanomeds. I never received them. Once they test me to design a suitable treatment program, they will find out."

"Won't they already know?" asked Aurelia, voicing Allegra's own question. "They would have tested your blood to discover you have this cancer."

Jocasta nodded. "Yes. It's likely they may have progressed to the next level already, but there are strict privacy laws in this time. They will not move forward without my permission, and I can only withhold it for so long."

"What is it you need me to do?" whispered Aurelia.

"Take her with you, Mother Aurelia," Jocasta begged, her grip on Aurelia's hands tightening. "Save her for me."

Jocasta moved to sit upright as she let out a soft sob. She looked away, to the window again and her eyes glistened, this time tears falling down her cheeks unchecked.

Then she drew a shuddering breath and gripped Aurelia's arm, staring at the old Pythia, her gaze filled with steel, and so much agony. "Please. There is a possibility that I will make it through. I will submit, let them try to figure out why I never got the nanomeds. But if I should choose that course of action, then the baby cannot be around. Either way, she cannot stay with me."

Aurelia nodded, her shoulders sagging. "They would test her to see if her blood, too, contains that anomaly. And they would discover that she doesn't."

"And it gets worse." The silence in the room echoed, as though Aurelia knew by now that if Jocasta said it would get worse, then it would really be bad.

"Worse than not being able to receive medical care?" asked Aurelia sharply, even though her voice broke on the question.

Jocasta nodded. "In this time, the NGS has scientists and researchers who are investigating what gives the seers and the Pythias the ability to receive their visions. Some of the researchers believe the seers have access to an energy field that channels energies from all timelines, allowing them to see the future. And they have made some progress…narrowed it down to a particular gene sequence that our entire Pythian line bears. Once they do that test, they will know what I am, and I will no longer have control of my life. And should they test the baby, they will know she is the next Pythia. The only one alive in this timeline."

Aurelia let out a deep, weary sigh. "I must confess, my dear child, that when you sent out that call, I did not expect to hear such terrible news."

Jocasta smiled sadly, then wiped her eyes and sniffed. "To be honest, I had hoped I would be calling on the previous Pythias during the blessing, not asking for you to take my child away."

Allegra stiffened as she slowly began to understand who this woman was and why her name was so familiar.

Jocasta.

Aurelia straightened and patted Jocasta's hand, offering her a last moment of comfort. "Very well. I will do what is required. Where is the infant?"

"In the nursery. They will bring her by in the next few minutes." Jocasta pointed at the wall opposite her bed. "There, press the wall beside the painting. You can wait in the bathroom until they leave. They will not look inside."

Aurelia nodded and hurried to the wall, hesitating a moment before pressing the white wall beside a swirling geometric pattern that seemed to be alive with colors. The wall clicked, and a panel popped toward Aurelia, a door hidden so neatly in the wall that you would never have known it was there.

The old Pythia entered the small space, depriving Allegra of her view of Jocasta. She hadn't realized how the sight of the woman would affect her, and even more so being unable to see her as Aurelia waited until someone entered the room, the sound of wheels rolling on tiles filtering into the bathroom.

Moments later, after the nurse had left, Aurelia exited the bathroom and paused to stare down at the sleeping child. She lay inside a white egg-shaped crib, staring around the room and smiling as though she could see everything around her.

Aurelia lifted the child from the bassinet and laid her in Jocasta's arms, stepping away as the mother said her farewells to her daughter.

After a few moments, during which Jocasta planted hundreds of kisses on the little infant's plump face, Aurelia said softly, "Will you send me a message when you are well, my dear child? Perhaps we could return the babe once you are back on your feet?"

Jocasta nodded, her eyes shining with unshed tears. She blinked a few times and then said, "I will send word. But if I don't, it will be because the danger is too high. Or because..."

She didn't need to complete the sentence. Allegra knew what she'd been about to say. Only Jocasta's death would be the reason she wouldn't call Aurelia again.

Allegra wasn't sure how she felt about the scene she was witness to. Aurelia was about to take a baby away from her mother, and something about the whole thing touched Allegra deep within her soul, as though she knew that it had something to do with herself.

She wanted to know so much more about what Aurelia knew, but all Allegra could do now was to watch and wait, and hope that one of the two would reveal a little more information. Still, Allegra was frustrated.

Swallowing hard, Allegra forced herself to continue to pay attention. At last Jocasta relinquished the child, the tears falling down her cheeks as Aurelia swaddled the baby tightly. "Take care of her for me, Mother Aurelia," Jocasta whispered.

"I will, child. Your mother would be most proud of you Jocasta. Cathenna had always spoken highly of you, her eldest daughter. She'd hoped that perhaps one day you would have been there to take over the reins from her."

Jocasta shrugged, a deep agony in her eyes. "It was a dangerous time for mother, especially with *him* dogging her every move. It pains me to know that he's decimated our line, that he has almost succeeded in achieving his goal, to kill us all, to end our line once and for all."

"He will not succeed, my child. We will prevail. We will keep every Pythia safe from his clutches. I will swear to that. On my own life, I will swear."

Jocasta struggled to produce a grateful smile. "I know you will. Thank you for doing this for me, Mother."

Aurelia straightened, and the child in her arms let out a low gurgling cry. Jocasta's instant response was a surge of tears, and Aurelia sighed. "I'm sorry, Jocasta. I must leave. I am already feeling the strain of the joining. It's best I go before the link collapses."

Jocasta nodded and stared at the baby for a pained second. Aurelia relented, taking the child back to her mother. She held the baby before Jocasta, close enough for her to place a gentle kiss on her child's forehead.

Then Aurelia stood back, holding the child close to her chest now. "Farewell, Jocasta. Take care of yourself, and I want to hear back from you soon. Please, for the sake of your child, I beg of you, do not give up on her, or on us. We will make every effort to come back to help you."

Jocasta nodded, her face solemn now as realization set in, as she faced head-on what she'd done. Desperation filled her eyes, grief an almost tangible feeling as she stared longingly at her child.

Just before Aurelia stepped away, she paused and turned toward Jocasta. "I almost forgot. The child's name?"

Jocasta let out a low sob, then shifted on the bed and slid open the drawer of her nightstand. She retrieved a piece of paper and held it out to Aurelia. "Her birth certificate, just in case she does return to this time."

With a nod, Aurelia took the document and glanced down at to read the name. Then, clutching the baby close, she stepped away, her form shimmering. But even as Aurelia disappeared and the sight of the hospital room and the grieving woman sitting along on the white bed faded, Allegra's mind was struggling to comprehend the name she'd just read.

"Allegra Jocasta Damaskos."

Allegra sucked in a shocked breath at the name.

Jocasta was her mother?

And she'd given Allegra up?

But the one thing that stood out the most in Allegra's mind was that Jocasta had confirmed the year in which Allegra had been born, a hundred years in the future.

CHAPTER 5

*A*llegra's body shook as she came back to consciousness, her lungs were near to exploding from the agony of holding her breath for so long—longer than she thought was humanly possible.

She kicked out, even though the action seemed far away, as though someone else was moving for her. Her body began to rise from the water, lifted by a force certainly not belonging to Allegra.

She shifted her head and found her savior.

Xales held onto Allegra's waist, gripping gently. Allegra's head lolled but she became more aware of her surroundings, and for some odd reason she no longer felt as though her lungs were about to explode.

Was it possibly because she was dying? Or perhaps already dead?

Allegra would have laughed at the thought had she been able to. Instead, she focused on remaining still and curling her free arm beneath the belt around Xales' neck.

As Allegra drew closer to the surface, pinpricks of light

filtered through the water, torches, and flashlights from the boats above her brightening the murky depths.

Divers were submerged and searching the water, two turning to spot Allegra almost simultaneously. Allegra tugged her arm from the boar's shoulder and curled closer to his back as he swam for the surface. The divers floated and watched Allegra and her boar familiar go by, their expressions somewhat dazed.

Had she had the strength to be amused she would have smiled.

Allegra's head broke the surface, and she felt herself pushed higher as Xales thrust her above water level toward the extended hands reaching for Allegra.

Warm arms encircled her waist and pulled her onto the deck where she dripped streams of water in puddles at her feet. Blankets were thrown around her shoulders, a warm cup of tea placed between her hands. Someone guided her to a chair, while another voice yelled to call the divers back on board.

And a few voices cried out in shock, claiming they'd seen a boar submerged in the water

Allegra blinked and wiped her eyes with her free hand as Max drew to her side and sat beside her on a low crate.

When she looked up, she saw relief, joy too, but both emotions were overshadowed by fury, and her heart sank. Not that she was afraid of his anger.

No, it was more because she was exhausted and she didn't think she'd be capable of standing up for herself. Right now, she just gave in and slumped against him, her head on his chest, feeling the stiffness of the muscles in his neck and shoulders.

When he finally relaxed, she knew she'd won—if only for the interim. The man wouldn't let go of the matter, not until he'd received her acknowledgment that she'd been wrong to come to Mranma in spite of his discouragement.

He'd better be ready to wait forever.

VOICES DRIFTED around Allegra as her body slowly warmed, and the shuddering of her limbs lessened. She was sitting beside a crate on the deck, under the inky black starlit sky, very much aware that deep beneath her was the boat that had just sunk, taking with it a handful of slavers.

Allegra found she felt not an iota of sympathy for those odious men.

Athena had come by a number of times, changing Allegra's blankets for warmer, drier ones, replacing her sodden pants and sweater with identical dry ones from their backup stock, plying her with cups of tea. The woman had performed each duty with an abundance of care, while still simmering with disapproval— perhaps not the same as Max's anger, but still something Allegra would need to overcome.

When Max finally came up to Allegra, the determination on his face told her in no uncertain terms that she wasn't going to be able to avoid him any longer.

Allegra got to her feet—clad now in warm, dry socks and boots—unable to suppress a long sigh. Max gave her a short nod and turned on his heel, entering the ship and leading Allegra to the captain's meeting room, a tiny space with a boardroom table only large enough to seat eight people elbow-to-elbow, with only a few centimeters between the chairs and the wall behind them.

Max waited only for Athena to enter the room before closing the door firmly behind him. Allegra chose a seat as far from the door as possible, mostly in order to be able to watch Max and gauge his reactions—not that predicting his behavior would help her at all.

She found it odd that she was so concerned with the feelings and mood of the other two occupants in the room, odd that she would be so sensitive to their specific fears. And Allegra wondered if it was wise at all to be so invested in the emotions of others, especially considering the nature of her role in this world.

Someday she may tell either—or both—of these people that

their lives would be coming to a conclusion sooner than they'd expected.

She did not want to see that day. Ever.

Allegra straightened in her seat now as Max turned to face her, the look in his eyes making her own jaw clench.

"What in Apollo's name was that stunt you pulled?" he asked, bending forward to place his palms on the table. His eyes flashed as he glared at her and she wanted to tell him that he should tone down the fury if he wanted to keep Xales from ripping him to pieces.

But she didn't speak, choosing to wait until Max had said his piece because she knew he wasn't done.

"You were supposed to stay on deck, Allegra," Max said while Athena looked on, her features schooled to reveal absolutely nothing of what she was thinking. Max shook his head. "How are we meant to protect you if you refuse to respect our security protocols?"

Allegra opened her mouth to speak, but Max took a breath and scrunched up his eyes, missing her intention.

"You agreed to stay on deck with us. To remain with either Athena or myself. If you had, you wouldn't have almost died down there."

"We're meant to be a team when we're in the field, Allegra," Athena said at last, her voice soft, but no less upset. "If we cannot rely on our team members, we are endangering all our lives."

Allegra lifted her hand, but Max cut her off again. "Do you have any idea how terrified we were? You disappear, the damn ship sinks, and there's no sign of you anywhere. We sent a team down, Athena and I both searched the ship. Nothing."

Allegra frowned now and snapped, "Hold on a moment. What do you mean you searched? There wouldn't have been enough time for that. I was barely down there for ten minutes," she looked at each of their faces, scowling at them for throwing everything out of proportion.

Max and Athena shared a look of confused horror, then the demigod turned to meet Allegra's eyes. "You were down there for forty-eight minutes and thirty-three seconds. We searched the entire ship and found nothing. How you're even alive, I'm not entirely sure," she said, shaking her head, confusion clouding her eyes.

Allegra sat back, biting her lip as she thought it over. Had she lost all that time that she'd spent with Aurelia in Jocasta's hospital room? Second for second? That would have been unusual given that her split-second flashes often contained minutes or even hours of visions.

Then Max sank into the seat opposite her, letting out a defeated sigh. "Fine. What happened?" he asked, raising an eyebrow, clearly curious though no less angry.

Allegra hid a grin. "We got the refugees off the ship, but one of the older men stopped me before he got onto the boat. He insisted his daughter was still inside, along with another little girl. I just reacted. I knew I had to find them, to save them, especially since I knew that ship was going down any second."

Max shook his head. "We saved so many people, Allegra. It wasn't your responsibility to save those girls."

Allegra's brow furrowed. "When you see the faces I see in my visions and feel the emotions I access, then you can tell me what my responsibility is or isn't," Allegra said, her words turning to a low growl as she stabbed her finger on the table in front of her. "If you saw the desperation in that father's eyes, you would have known I had no choice but to help him find her. You'd evacuated the ship, and everyone was already on the boats. If we had waited any longer, the chances of saving those children would have been low to nil, so I took the opportunity and went to look for them. I did not have the time to waste."

Neither Athena nor Max spoke, making it somewhat unclear as to their emotions. Allegra took a slow, even breath and continued, "I found the girl, both the girls, actually. They were in the captain's cabin, handcuffed to the bed." Allegra paused to gauge first Athena's and then Max's expressions. Both were now somewhat subdued. "I released the girls, got them out of the cabin, but that was when the ship tilted, and the door slammed shut on me and then jammed. The girls tried to get it open, but it wouldn't budge."

Max pursed his lips. "Those girls were terrified that you were going to die. They swam to the surface and reported the incident, we got a diving party together and came down looking for you. How you even survived so long is a miracle."

Allegra leaned forward, elbows on the table. "Air pocket in the captain's quarters. I used that to keep breathing, but eventually, I ran out of air."

"So you used the air pocket to stay alive for *forty* odd minutes?" asked Athena, her eyes wide as she faced Allegra.

"Sort of."

"It's a yes or no answer. No *maybe* option," Max said, his eyes narrowing.

Allegra's shoulders drooped. "You do have a point. And I will elaborate later." She took a deep breath and then got to her feet. "Now, I need to speak to the families who are waiting out there for me and then we need to get out of here."

Max gave a sharp bob of his head in reluctant agreement, though his eyes still remained hard as he rose and opened the boardroom door. Allegra knew neither of them was done ripping pieces off her hide, but she was fine with that. She'd give them another opportunity when they got home to Argentina.

Until then, they'd just have to wait.

CHAPTER 6

*A*llegra exited the captain's boardroom and approached the open door to the deck. The people they'd rescued were milling around the space, many covered in blankets, huddling together for warmth or comfort. The night had grown cooler now, the temperature dropping, made worse by being on the water.

A few refugees about on their own, some smoking, others drinking the strong cane spirits offered by the captain.

That Captain Ailrut had been so generous with his stores had nothing whatsoever to do with the man's generosity, rather more to do with the generosity of the NGS government's aide coffers.

The Mranman ambassador to the NGS Capitol had declined to comment or to engage in negotiations regarding the so-called traitors who had attempted to run out of their own country, completely disregarding the reasons for their escape.

As Allegra walked outside, the groups turned to watch her, some wary, others with expressions of gratitude. Still, most appeared to be edgy, ready to flee if anyone spoke too loudly. A small family group was gathered closest to the door, and Allegra approached them first, recognizing the man as the father who'd begged for his daughter to be found.

The girl was nowhere to be seen, and Allegra assumed she was inside the ship, resting—especially considering how terrified the child had been. Allegra didn't want to think about what the captain had done with the girls, a part of her hoping he'd sold them to the highest bidders who'd have paid steeply for virgin slaves.

The father looked up and smiled, revealing a mouth missing a few teeth. Those remaining had mostly rotted through, and would likely follow the same route as their counterparts.

He got to his feet and began to speak, his language alien to her. Allegra shook her head and held up a hand before glancing around the deck. She spotted Kyaswa, one of the crewman who leaned against the side of the ship, the smoke from his cigarette curling around in a hazy cloud. He'd been introduced earlier as able to translate if the need arose.

Allegra beckoned the man, who took a long pull on his cigarette, then stubbed the still burning butt on the deck, grinding it down with his heel. Kyaswa's expression remained bland as he sauntered over, taking his time as if to make it clear that Allegra was not his boss.

She bit her tongue and forced a neutral smile on her face. "Kyaswa, could you be so kind as to translate for me?"

The man eyed her for a moment then tugged his cap down over his eyes and waited.

"Could you ask them how they came to be on the ship?" Allegra shifted to look at Athena, giving her a pointed look before flicking a glance at their unwilling translator. "Athena, could you record the interview please?"

The fact that the proceedings were now a formal process seemed to draw a more serious attitude from Kyaswa who straightened, his expression going from bland and uninterested to serious. He proceeded to relate Allegra's question to the father who replied haltingly, his eyes filling with tears.

"We work hard, my wife, my children, me. But we cannot afford the landlord's rent and taxes. So we tried to find a way to go to a better place."

Allegra frowned. "Taxes?"

The man nodded as Kyaswa relayed the question. "The landlord, he asks for sixty percent of our earnings. But we pay rent first and then the tax, so there is not much left to buy food and to pay for school and clothing."

Anger simmered within Allegra, and she shared a glance with Athena. No wonder the Mranman government was unwilling to assist the NGS operation to save these people.

"How did you end up on the ship?"

The old man's face darkened. "We heard about the captain Uzana who will take you across to Indus for a fee. We came to see him, and he said yes. We paid, and he took us on board. But things were not as he promised."

Allegra frowned then nodded, "Please go on. What happened when you got on board?"

"Captain Uzana separated the families. He sent the men to a separate hold, and the women to another. He took the young girls, to keep them upstairs. He said to protect them from the other men, but I was not so sure. We kept asking where they were but none of his men would tell us. Until one of them got drunk and laughed at me when I asked when I can see my daughter. He said she already fetched a big price on the slave market and that when we docked her new master would come to fetch her and we would never see her again. He laughed at us, calling us fools for thinking we could escape and that now we were doomed to spend a lifetime as slaves never to be free again."

"Did he tell you where the captain was sending you to work?"

The old man nodded after Kyaswa relayed the question. "The old women to the sweatshops in Laos. And the men to the gold and copper mines in Hpkant. Those businesses were banned, but they still keep going, only nobody knows because the workers are all slaves."

Athena grunted. "Legal employees would have to be registered in order to pay taxes to their localities. Slave labor would have answered that particular problem. So they wouldn't have shut down completely."

Allegra took a deep breath and looked at the old man who began to speak again, Kyaswa relaying his sentences one at a time, "I thank you. My family thanks you. You helped when everyone had gone from the ship. You risked your life to save my daughter. We owe you our lives."

The man bowed repeatedly, and Allegra reached out to grasp his hands in hers. "There is no need to thank me. I did what had to be done. We are all here to help each other." She smiled at the man whose eyes filled with tears again.

Stepping away, Allegra looked over at Max who'd remained at the doorway, the captain standing at his side, expression shadowed.

"Max, can we see to it that these people are taken to Indus as they wished?"

Max nodded. "I suppose Aulus wouldn't mind if the refugees ended up elsewhere. And I'm sure Sonali would be happy to take them." As he headed back inside the cabin with the captain in tow, Max called over his shoulder, "Let me make a couple of calls. Then we need to get out of here."

Allegra spent a few moments speaking to the gathered families who wished to thank her in person. Though all she wanted to do was to run back inside and hide, disliking the idea of accepting praise in any form, she forced herself to stay with them, just until they were satisfied.

CHAPTER 7

*L*ord Severus Langcourt smiled at the man who stood before him.

Unlike Severus's own nondescript coloring and distinct lack of hair, golden-haired Illaris Von Demme was a perfect example of mortal beauty. And a top scientist, a man who knew physics better than anyone else in history. And this man now stood in Langcourt's office, ready to extol the virtues of his latest invention—an advanced iteration of a core mechanism that would successfully power Langcourt's sonic emission device.

Time had begun to haunt Langcourt, the reflection that met him in his mirror every morning was a constant reminder that he needed Allegra more than ever before.

He'd taken to the family hideaway on Akída, a small island off the coast of Alkebulan from where he'd been putting both short- and long-term plans in place.

Now, Langcourt turned to the scientist, folding his arms, biceps bulging. "So, Dr. Von Demme, when can you demonstrate the efficacy of your device?"

Von Demme stiffened, his affronted scowl implying that the man had expected to be taken at his word. Then his shoulders relaxed, and he forced a smile onto his face. "Of course, Lord Langcourt. I'm available as soon as you have time."

Langcourt smiled. Of course, Von Demme would shift his position when money was involved. That was the main reason Langcourt had approached the man. Too many of the best physicists available were already contracted to medical institutes, hospitals and governmental organization making it near impossible for Langcourt to solicit their skills for his project.

Probably the only reason Von Demme had responded to Langcourt's communications was the man was out of a job.

With a firm nod, Langcourt got to his feet. "I will contact you with a time and a location. I will also arrange transportation for you to the site."

Von Demme stammered, hesitating before also rising to his feet. "But, I thought..."

"Oh, I do apologize if I gave you the impression that I would need you to demonstrate immediately. I'm a little tied up right now—appointments for the next few hours—so it's quite impossible to drag myself away without upsetting a great many people."

Von Demme nodded though his dissatisfaction was clear. "It's quite alright, Langcourt. I'll be ready when you need me."

The door to the hotel room opened, and Roquefort walked in, the sight of the man startling the physicist who shrank away as Langcourt's assistant neared the desk.

"Ah, Roquefort. Would you be so kind as to show Doctor Von Demme out? We'll be seeing much of the Doctor very soon, so please take good care of him." Langcourt waved the pair away and sat at his desk, pulling the stack of files closer and selecting three of them. He barely looked up as Roquefort led the nervous doctor out.

The door shut solidly behind them, and Langcourt sat back, heaving a sigh of relief. The interview process had been supremely tedious, more so now that Langcourt had begun to tire easily as age slowly began to catch up to him.

He tugged open the top drawer of his desk and retrieved a hand-held mirror, using it to study the deep lines on his face, the wrinkles around his eyes, the faintest hint of a cataract in his left eye. His skin had grown papery thin, a smattering of liver spots now covering his hands, and his bones had developed a persistent ache, where every movement had begun to elicit a wince.

Without the life force of the Pythia, Langcourt would continue to ail. He disliked this dance he performed, this elaborate attempt to entice her to him. But it was a necessary evil, a step in the process that, though painful, was the way to his final success.

Killing the Pythia Allegra.

a few minutes later when the families had drifted back to their huddles and had left Allegra alone with Athena, Max hurried out of the cabin.

"We're good to go. Queen Sonali is only too happy to accept the families we have on board, and the captain has been kind enough to agree to take them over." Max's cool smile indicated that the captain had certainly not behaved out of the goodness of his heart.

Allegra smiled and thanked the man, and was about to enter the cabin to look for something to eat when a shot rang out.

Spinning on her heel she ducked low, grabbing hold of a young boy who was attempting to peer over the port-side balustrade in the direction from which the shot had originated. Thankfully, no further shots were fired, and after a few tense moments, a man's voice rang across the bay, his tone filled with authority, impatience, and a touch of anger.

"What is he saying?" Allegra hissed at Kyaswa, who was sprawled on the deck, legs spread-eagled, puffing away on a newly lit cigarette.

"He says we are not to move or they will kill us all," the man replied, smirking around his cigarette.

Gasps rang out across the deck, and the families huddled even tighter together as the man with the loudspeaker sent out more instructions.

Kyaswa chuckled again, then added, "He says 'Hand over the traitors, and I will let the ship leave the harbor safely.'"

Max had obtained his own loudspeaker and had edged toward the balustrade. He was now opening a dialog with the man on the shore, one which Allegra suspected would end up going nowhere. Which meant the refugees needed to get to safety immediately.

After a few moments of tense discussion, Max shut off his megaphone and headed toward the ladder to the left of the wheelhouse.

"Max? What are you doing?" called Allegra, her heart jumping.

"I have to go over to talk to them."

"And what if they don't let you return alone?"

"They won't want to cause an international incident, especially not if they deliberately broke parley."

Allegra snorted. "I wasn't aware this was a battle."

Athena got to her feet and headed toward Max. "I'm going with you," she said firmly.

Max shook his head and glared at the two women staring at him. "No. I'll go alone. The last thing I need is to give them more hostages. If things go pear-shaped, you can all still get to safety. Get the refugees out of here."

"Max!" Allegra yelled out, but the man hurried to the ladder and swung over the edge.

Funny how he was endangering himself in much the same way as Allegra had, but thought it was a perfectly reasonable action to take.

Max paused on the ladder and met Allegra's eyes for a moment. "I'll be fine. Athena, cover me just in case. I'm meeting them on the beach." He nodded at the small island with its narrow strip of sand a hundred meters behind him. "Not too far, but I want the engines running."

Allegra grunted, about to say something nasty, when Athena scuttled off the deck into the wheelhouse. Allegra glared at Max who hung over the side of the ship, his back to the small group of men who were slowly gathering on the beach.

Military types, red and khaki uniforms, guns at their hips, rifles in their arms at the ready. A portly man held a pair of binoculars to his eyes, and Allegra wondered who he was trying to locate on the ship—Max or the refugees.

Athena returned moments later with the long weapons-bag. Unzipping it, she held a rifle up to Max, but he shook his head. "Agreement is I go unarmed."

"Are you insane? They're all armed, Max," Allegra snapped. "Even the big guy has a pistol on his belt. How can you agree to go in unarmed?"

"Parley, Allegra. I called it in, and I told Major Guri as much. He's sworn to abide by the agreement." Max's jaw tightened, and he began to lower himself down the ladder to the small boat that floated below, tethered to the ladder with a frayed rope.

"Wait," called out the father who'd expressed so much appreciation for the saving of his daughter's life. "I go." The man motioned with his hands to indicate accompanying Max.

"No, there is no need." Max shook his head.

"Yes…" the man said, nodding vigorously as he made a rowing motion with his arms, then increased the pace to imply getting away fast.

Max sighed and waved the man forward. As the old man moved past Allegra, she grabbed his arm and pointed a finger at him. "Wait." She turned on her heel, hurried to the translator and grabbed the hat from the man's head, then waved at the loosely tied scarf around his neck.

He lifted an eyebrow, but complied without resistance. When

Allegra eyed his cigarette, he removed it from between his lips and handed it over. She gave him a grateful smile and handed all three items to the old man.

"Put it on. You're a sailor."

Though the man hesitated, he too obeyed, jamming the cap onto his head, pulling the peak low across his brow. He tied the scarf, which reeked of smoke and sweat and gasoline, with no indication of its original color left, then popped the cigarette between his lips.

Then, without another word, he followed Max down to the boat and proceeded to row them the hundred or so meters over to the shore. Every time the oar hit the water, Allegra's heart jumped.

Beside Allegra, Athena loaded her rifle and rested the barrel on the port-side handrail, aimed at the beach. Though tempted to emulate the demigod immediately, Allegra had one thing to do first.

Glancing over at the little boat as it neared halfway to the shore, Allegra said, "I have something to do, but I'll be right back."

Despite the arch look Athena responded with, Allegra didn't clarify. She duck-walked over to the door to the ship as fast as she could, and from the threshold she beckoned the three families, urgently motioning for them to go inside while also holding a finger to her lips. They obeyed, crawling toward her despite the expressions of fear on their faces.

"Poor people. They're terrified of going back inside a ship. Not that I blame them. I'm not too thrilled myself," Allegra said to Athena as she watched over them.

Athena grunted from her spot a meter away from the door. "I don't blame any one of you. But getting them to safety is the smartest option right now. Who knows where this will end."

Allegra slipped inside the narrow corridor to find Alrait rushing over to the group, waving his arms in an attempt to herd them down into the hold but some of the women, as well as both the girls Allegra had saved, began to cry, shaking with terror.

Allegra waved over to the man. "Leave them. Is there some-place up above where we can keep them for a short while?"

Captain Alrait shook his head, his eyes flashing as he glared at Allegra. "There is only my private cabin, and the boardroom. They have to—"

Allegra lifted a hand. "Thank you, captain. I'll have one family use your quarters, and the other two can use the boardroom. Once we're out of the harbor, we can relocate them."

With that she turned and motioned for the family with the three small children to follow her, glancing over at Athena and jerking her chin at the other two families. A mere minute later, Allegra had returned from setting the family up in the captain's cabin, and the rest of the refugees had been set up in the tiny boardroom having tipped the table up and set it against the wall to open up a bit more floor space for ten people.

Allegra made her way back outside and met Athena beside the handrail where the demigod watched the boat reaching the shore. Allegra reached for the bag, grabbed a rifle, prepped and checked it, ignoring Athena's sideways glance. She didn't care if the demigod approved or not.

The more cover Max had, the higher the chances of him escaping the parley with his sorry neck intact.

CHAPTER 9

*W*ith her barrel positioned on the handrail, Allegra sighted Max as he approached the major, and watched as the two spoke. The major stood straight-backed, his features hard and shadowed by the darkness. A few soldiers held torches which threw undulating light and shadows into the occupants of the beach, making it difficult for Allegra to read what was going on.

The ten minutes of discussion that ensued felt like eons ticking by one second at a time and Allegra crouched, barely conscious of the strain on her thighs.

"It doesn't look good," she murmured to Athena, watching the line of Max's spine as he spoke to the Mranma representative.

"What makes you think that? We really shouldn't be presuming the worst," Athena replied, doing nothing to hide her ironic smirk.

Allegra snorted. "I know Max. And I am only reading it as I see it. I would much rather presume the worst and be prepared, than be light-hearted and positive only to get killed in the process."

"Allegra?" said Athena, her tone low and even.

"Yes, Athena?" Allegra replied without taking her eyes off of Max as he took a step back, indicating their parley had come to an end.

"I was being facetious," the demigod replied, chuckling softly.

Allegra flicked her a brief glance. "Oh, I see," she replied, eyes already on the beach. Then Allegra stiffened, training her rifle on the shoreline. As she sighted the armed soldiers who watched Max climb into his boat, Allegra flipped the safety off, relieved to hear Athena's own click of preparation.

From the corner of her vision, she saw the old man begin to row the boat back to the *Yakshi*, but something turned over in Allegra's stomach as she watched the soldiers, as the general motioned to his men, as the two closest to the shore drew their rifles to their shoulders.

"Athena?"

"Yes, my lady?"

"Maim, not kill, okay?"

Athena grunted in reply.

Max was fifty meters from the shore when the first soldier's finger began to squeeze his trigger. Awareness sharpened and Allegra felt each second sift by as though time had slowed. She took aim, and tapped her trigger just as the sniper pulled his. Both shots echoed simultaneously, so in tandem that it would have appeared as though only one shot had been fired.

"Well done," muttered Athena grudgingly as the two women watched the soldier who was now staring at his empty hands in shock, face crumpling in a warped combination of shock and embarrassment.

For a few seconds, silence reigned as the gathered troops on the shore turned to stare at the rifle which now lay four feet from the sniper.

Then the major yelled out, and the soldiers burst into motion, scattering into the underbrush. Max had grabbed an oar and was helping to row, the little boat increasing in speed and drawing closer to safety, only now angling toward the ship's bow.

"He's going around. Lay down cover fire." Athena called out instructions even though only the two women were bothered to do anything.

"Captain Alrait," yelled Allegra as the first of the shots were fired from the trees beyond the beach, thankfully falling short of Max's boat. The man merely grunted in reply, which stirred Allegra's fury. "Can you get this boat moving? And we could use some help here to cover the Commander!" she called as she peppered the beach in front of the tree-line with a hail of bullets.

"I'm sorry, my lady. My men would rather not fire on Mranman soldiers. We will never be able to work in these waters again." Alrait's tone was half amused, half cold, as though the sight of two women firing on a troop of trained soldiers was a funny sight to behold.

"Captain, please understand that you are, this minute, making a choice. A life-sentence for deliberately endangering the life of a high-ranking NGS official or a substantial reward for helping us free these refugees and for ensuring the safety of that high-ranking NGS official."

The demigod growled. "Or how about a death sentence for you and your crew if the Pythia dies in the firefight?" yelled Athena, impatience almost palpable as her voice cracked on the last word.

Although Allegra did register the *Yakshi's* engines firing and the vessel beginning to edge forward slowly, she didn't look behind her to see if the captain had complied with helping them cover Max's escape. She was too busy taking aim at a soldier who rolled a heavy machine-gun into a clearing in the trees.

The soldier had barely set the weapon down when Allegra fired, the bullet slamming into the man's palm as he reached for the trigger. Allegra's bullet then penetrated the trigger mechanism, jamming the weapon.

A situation that became very clear as a second soldier closed in to take over. He turned the heavy barrel toward the ship, and then began to struggle with the trigger.

Max's boat was no longer visible from where Allegra sat, but at this point, all she cared about was keeping the soldiers busy until Max was safe. Beside her, Athena was busy firing at a line of snipers in the trees, taking them out one at a time even while she rained bullets into the trees beyond them.

Allegra prepared to fire on the machine-gun, but the weapon exploded instead, sending a shower of bullets in all directions.

"Well done, Allegra," said Athena with a loud whoop. "Not safe yet, though. They will come back. I'd bet your new bronze corset on that."

Allegra snorted then chuckled. "That is no bet. There is movement in the trees."

The explosion had sent the troops on the beach into disarray as they ducked for cover and fled into the trees, but they were not about to leave without a fight.

"IR on," Allegra said softly. She much preferred using her own vision to aim and fire, but with the soldiers obscured by the dense foliage, it was nearly impossible to see where the next barrage of bullets was likely to erupt.

Allegra had barely slipped the rifle's sighting mechanism to IR vision when she detected movement. "Co-ordinated attack within the tree-line," she said.

"I see it. I have the six on the left," replied Athena.

The *Yakshi* was now moving fast, and a shout from the aft section confirmed their men were safe and boarding. Max's feet had barely touched the deck before he was yelling out instructions. "Captain, can we have full power *now*? We cannot delay in case the major returns with heavier weapons."

Oddly enough, the captain complied without resistance, and the small ship surged forward just as Athena and Allegra dominated the second attack. They fired on the soldiers even before the small troop had begun firing.

The *Yakshi* surged ahead, gliding along narrow channels between the hundreds of little islands around them. Alrait remained at the wheel, surly and silent as the ship left the shallow water and headed into the deeper ocean.

Allegra and Athena hurried inside the wheelhouse where they listened to Max alerting the Indus coastguards of their arrival and requisitioned air support.

Allegra had just stepped back to settle herself onto the captain's low chart desk when the window where she'd just been standing exploded, sending shards of glass in every direction.

"Down," yelled Max, as a wall panel exploded behind him.

Alrait began to holler out orders while Max yelled for a weapon. While Athena supplied him with firepower, Allegra slid toward the window, the low thrum of an aircraft grating against her nerves.

"Incoming aircraft, Max. And something tells me that's not the air-support you requested."

Max growled as a second hail of fire ripped through the wheelhouse. He surged forward and fired on the helicopter as it rounded the ship and hovered a hundred meters off the port bow.

"These people are beginning to get on my nerves," Allegra growled. In one smooth move, she drew her rifle, took aim, and fired. Then she turned to face Max. "Can we get out of here now, please?"

She was halfway across the threshold and into the interior passage to the cabins when the helicopter exploded, the fireball lighting the shocked faces of the three occupants of the wheelhouse. The captain let out a shocked squeal—the reaction something Allegra wasn't sure was entirely complimentary.

Max and Athena simply stared at the remains of the helicopter as it fell into the ocean. Alrait continued to guide the

Yakshi past the still burning fuel tanks, giving the detritus of the explosion a wide berth.

Max raised his eyebrows at the destruction, impressed as he gave a low whistle.

Athena let out a disgusted growl, turning to face Allegra, eyes sparking. "Could you possibly just leave *some* of the fun stuff to us?" she asked, her expression a perfect blend of annoyance and admiration.

Allegra shrugged. "Sorry. Must have been a fluke."

"Fluke? My furry hindquarters," Athena muttered, folding her arms while Max merely watched the two women in amusement. All appeared well in the end, and it was now time to go home.

Probably also time for a mortal and a demigod to yell at an oracle.

CHAPTER 10

*A*fter what seemed like an interminable length of time, Max let out a deep sigh.

Captain Alrait had made it to the shores of Chennai, and delivered his grateful human cargo into the welcoming arms of Queen Sonali's refugee care officials.

Allegra had been thanked and offered accommodations to freshen up and prepare for their flight back, but she'd declined, much to the very clear relief of both Max and Athena.

They'd been in the air now for an hour, in which time they'd showered, changed, and eaten their first decent meal in almost two days.

Now, Max's strained expression was a tad deflated—if more than a little exhausted—and considering he'd been furious and on the edge of his seat waiting to yell at Allegra for her recklessness, she wasn't surprised.

Despite knowing he was ready to give her a piece of his mind, she felt a pulsing of love toward the man. Any person who could care this much about the safety of a loved one was truly worth their weight in gold. The only problem was, Allegra quite liked being the mistress of her own destiny—however limited that may be when one considered the responsibility of her prophetic powers.

"I used the air pocket for probably ten minutes," Allegra was explaining, having taken up her tale from where she'd left off in the *Yakshi's* boardroom. "After that, I held my breath, then the ship slipped further, did a somersault and then landed. The shifting allowed me to open the cabin door, but I didn't make it to total freedom."

"What happened?" asked Max, his eyes darkening.

"I made it outside, but something hit me. Hard. I thought it may have been the chimney, but I couldn't be sure. Knocked the air out of my lungs. I thought I was going to die. My lungs just couldn't take it. And then I…."

"You what?"

Allegra let out a self-deprecating laugh. "It's going to sound far-fetched, ridiculous even."

Athena snorted. "Allegra, you get visions and predict the future," the woman said, an eyebrow raised.

Allegra let out a sigh. "The chimney knocked me aside, I ran out of air, and I passed out. When I opened my eyes, I was inside a hospital room. There were screens on the walls that looked like those new computers that were only just released in the NGS. But these were much more advanced. Glistening black and silver, small screens that showed bio signs, heartbeat, blood pressure."

"Hospital room?" asked Max.

Allegra nodded. "The patient was a woman, and when she looked up, she began to speak to me. But she wasn't addressing *me*. She was speaking to Aurelia, as though she'd called on her or summoned her. Perhaps she had done just that, but I just couldn't get my head around the thought.

"Even when Aurelia called her Jocasta, I still didn't connect the dots." Allegra met Max's shocked gaze as he rubbed his hand over his face. "She told Aurelia to take her baby away."

"This Jocasta? She gave her baby away to the Pythia Aurelia?

In a time where the technology was more advanced than now?" Athena seemed to be struggling with getting her head around the idea of Allegra's vision.

Allegra nodded. "Jocasta...had cancer but she mentioned being unable to seek treatment until her baby was taken to safety. She had two reasons—because once they ran the tests, they would identify her as being not of their time, and two because in this future they have discovered a genetic marker that indicates a person possesses powers, like seers or telepaths."

"So, Aurelia took this child with her? To a different time?" asked Athena, her brow knitted together.

Allegra nodded. "Yes. Aurelia agreed to take the baby. And Jocasta promised to send her a message when she was well. They made a pact to send the baby back to Jocasta when it was safe."

"I'm assuming Aurelia never did send back the child," Athena said, leaning back, tapping a finger on the worktable between them.

Allegra smiled. "No, Aurelia didn't, of that, I am one hundred percent certain."

"How can you be so certain? As it turns out, Aurelia was holding out on us. So many things she never told anyone."

Allegra leaned forward and rubbed her face. "I'm certain because I know where that baby is, and she's definitely not with Jocasta."

Athena sat back, her finger stilling its erratic movements. Then she snapped her gaze up and stared at Allegra. "*You* are that baby?"

Allegra nodded. "And I have the birth certificate to prove it."

Max cleared his throat, shared a brief glance with Athena, and then shifted his gaze to Allegra. "How do we know what your vision truly meant? What if it was just something you saw because of a heightened sense of fear, and not because it truly was a journey to a different time as it appeared to be to you?" Max's expression was tense, his brow furrowed with worry. His fingers gripped the edge of the table, knuckles white as he held his frustration with Allegra at bay.

She understood his emotional state, but his words still frustrated her. Allegra's lips formed a thin line, but she forced herself to remain calm, to breath in and out and to see his side of her story.

Also, she knew what Max was doing; he was trying to remain sensible in the face of her fantastic tale, throwing possibly more logical answers into the mix as options to consider. Allegra nodded slowly. "I suppose it could have been oxygen deprivation hallucinations, or a hysteria-related vision, brought on by fear, a mingling of what I want to know about who I am, and what I'd like my past to be."

Which was a lie simply because Allegra had never obsessed about her true origins. Even when she'd read the words on her birth certificate—found in the trunk in Aurelia's old bedroom— Allegra had never taken the existence of that piece of paper as though it were a window onto a life she should have lived, a life she'd lost because of various series of events.

Now, as Allegra studied her team, considering Max's words, Athena began to shake her head. "I'm not so sure it's all that wise to ignore what this vision says," the demigod said, her eyes dark with concern. She looked over at Max. "I understand what you're doing by questioning the validity of Allegra's vision, but we have other aspects that need to be questioned. And we owe it to Allegra to consider them as well."

"And what are these other aspects," asked Max as he leaned back against the seat and looked from Athena to Allegra. He didn't appear to be upset that the demigod was challenging him on his perceptions. In fact, he looked mildly curious.

Allegra herself was most interested in Athena's opinion, especially when she accepted that the demigod had only ever been supportive and protective, and had only ever considered Allegra's safety as paramount.

Athena took a deep breath and leaned forward, elbows resting on the table. "Even if we start out believing this to be a vision, there is the matter of Allegra's ability to hold her breath for thirty odd minutes. We know she's capable of just over three minutes, but anything more and I'd be worried. We've estimated a ten-minute length of time spent trapped inside the cabin before the ship rolled and Allegra managed to escape the vessel. There are still thirty minutes in which Allegra remained underwater—with no possible method of obtaining oxygen to ensure she remained alive."

"Unless Xales brought her a diver's oxygen tank, thus hood-winking us all?" offered Allegra with a smirk.

Her attempt at lightening the almost palpable tension inside the small boardroom resulted in Max's lip curling as a smile formed, a smile he suppressed quickly, defaulting to his standard serious mode.

Athena, on the other hand, remained scowling as she said, "One suggestion for such a situation is Allegra being physically transported to this vision, perhaps in an actual time-travel experience." Athena's words were spoken softly as she hesitated with each thought. It sounded preposterous when put into words, but the idea made more than a little sense to Allegra.

Max scoffed. "That's ridiculous." He shook his head, his amusement now tinged with disbelief.

Athena merely glanced at him with one eyebrow raised. "As ridiculous as a birth certificate to prove that Allegra is from the future?" asked Athena, her eyes flashing. Then she glanced briefly at Allegra, and spoke out of the side of her mouth, "We're still going to have a discussion regarding why you didn't tell me anything about this 'from the future' part of your past."

Allegra grinned.

"Anyway," Athena waved a hand in the air, "since our favorite oracle isn't capable of going into voluntary organic stasis, I propose we consider the time travel option for the moment, as an actuality. So how do we explain that you were there, but viewing the scene from Aurelia's point of view?"

Allegra sat back and blinked. "Because, maybe I *was* seeing it from her eyes, but was also sort of piggybacking on her spirit as it traveled to Jocasta? I'm not entirely sure this is something we can explain enough to make perfect sense right now."

Athena nodded. "There are many things that remain inexplicable."

Max grunted. "Fine. Let's consider this vision as a time jump. So what do we know for sure?" Max paused as he considered his words. "First, we know Jocasta was terminally ill. And we know Jocasta is Cathenna's daughter, sent there from the ancient past to protect her life."

"And we know that there may have been more than one oracle sent to different time periods."

"Oh?"

"Jocasta said that her sisters were sent away as well and she'd hoped to someday see them, although she wasn't sure she'd ever be able to."

"I see." Max frowned. "So Cathenna sent her daughters to different time periods to protect them from being murdered."

"Yes, and that would be Langcourt who killed Cathenna. She did have reason to believe they were in danger, that much we know. Which would justify her reason for sending her daughters away."

Max nodded. "So Cathenna knows there is a danger to the Pythias, sends her daughters away just in time. Then she's murdered by Langcourt's progenitor. And then, in the future, Jocasta discovers she is dying and calls for a Pythia to help, only the one oracle who responds is Aurelia."

Allegra nodded. "Perhaps Aurelia was the only one who knew that when she dies there would be nobody to take her place?"

"And a decision could have been made for Aurelia to take Jocasta's baby to her own time."

Athena sat forward. "This all implies that Aurelia would have known in advance that Jocasta was asking for someone to take her baby away."

Allegra nodded. "The Pythias, through the Oracle bloodline, have been able to communicate through the timelines. It's likely how Cathenna made her decisions on where to send her children. The oracles knew enough to be well aware that their children were all at risk. How would they have known that if not for the fact that they have access to each other through the timelines?"

"That makes sense. But, from what you have told me, the killers have not stopped killing the Oracles. Langcourt did, only recently, attempt to kill you, too."

"I suspect he may have been a little confused because he'd thought with Aurelia's passing there were no more oracles," Allegra tapped the table as she spoke.

"Maybe he thought you were an anomaly? Or the Pythia line emerging from out of thin air?"

Allegra chuckled. "I imagine that would have been most distressing to Langcourt."

"Not if he needed you dead for some specific reason?" muttered Max still rubbing his chin with his fingers. "Okay, let's say we accept everything so far. Now, the question we ask is how you ended up getting to the future without having performed any ritual to gain access?"

"Perhaps a god helped you get there?" offered Athena. Then her eyes brightened. "You were in the water. Perhaps it was Neptune?"

At the mention of the god's name, Allegra felt slightly ill. Neptune wasn't in the business of saving Allegra.

Killing her was more likely.

CHAPTER 11

*A*llegra paled, and she felt the pulsing of nausea and straightened.

Memories of that awful day when Allegra and her dearest friend in all the world had almost been killed when their boat had gone down in an unexpected storm, memories of a presence that had seemed determined to kill Allegra. Knowing even then that Neptune, god of the oceans had wanted to kill her.

Swallowing hard, she said, "I don't believe Neptune holds me in high enough regard that he would wish to protect my life."

Athena's jaw tightened, her brow creasing as she leaned forward a fraction. "How could you say that?" the demigod appeared affronted at the suggestion. "Neptune is known for his kindness, his love for humanity. He'd never hurt anyone, least of all an oracle."

Allegra let out a soft sigh. "I'm sorry. It's just that Neptune has tried to kill me already. He'd have succeeded if it hadn't been for Xales. Both Xenia and I would have drowned if the god of the oceans had succeeded."

Athena's eyes filled with tears. "I'm sorry. I didn't know. I just don't know how that's even possible. I can't fathom how Neptune would ever do such a thing," she said, her words trailing off in a whisper.

Allegra shrugged, trying and failing to remain emotionally detached. "Perhaps he's not as good as you think he is?" she said, even as she found her mind filled with images of black water surrounding her, pressing in on her senses, her ears throbbing with the sounds of muted screams, her own perhaps as terror ruled her reactions, as she drifted further and further away from the surface of the ocean.

"Or perhaps," said Athena, her voice tugging Allegra from the horrific experience, "there is more to the story than you know?"

Allegra's eyebrow quirked as she calmed enough to consider Athena's suggestion. "How so?" she asked softly, swallowing down her distress.

She knew she was merely humoring the demigod, her stomach churning as she faced the terrible fact that Athena's understanding of the god Neptune had been so very wrong. And at the fact that Allegra had been forced to ruin Athena's love for Neptune. It couldn't be that much different to having to reveal to a child that their parent was a killer.

Athena smiled sadly. "I know that your experience with Neptune may have been affected by something, perhaps an outside influence. You've had obstacles placed in your path every step of the way since the moment Max found you. What if there are forces out there that want to ensure you do not trust Neptune for some reason?" Then she let out a long, ragged breath and ran her hands through her hair, mussing her usually neatly combed ponytail. "Or maybe I am entirely wrong here, and my own perception has been flawed all along."

Allegra sighed and leaned against the window, looking out at the clouds and the endless blue sky. "I've always loved the water. It has always been the one place in which I could feel at peace. And ever since that moment when the *Qurux* went down and Xenia and I almost died—when Neptune tried to kill us—I've been terrified of the water. I stay far away from it, even though I'm desperate to be within it."

"Could there be something about that peace you feel while within the water that perhaps someone understands better than you?" asked Max, his voice almost startling Allegra. When she glanced over at him, he gave her a soft, apologetic smile. "Perhaps the water gives you a certain clarity?"

Allegra stilled as she recalled her experiences inside the pool back at her villa in Venara Hills.

Athena rapped the table with her fingernails. "Right from the beginning, when the first Sybils were channeling prophecies and the words of the gods, water was always used as the medium for inducing visions, or at least inducing the oracle, in either the Delphian or more standard-issue seers."

Allegra let out a soft laugh as she glanced at Athena. "Standard issue seers. That's funny. I wonder what Corina would—" Allegra's smile withered, and her heart clenched as Corina's cheerful smile drifted before her.

"Allegra?" Max's voice penetrated her haze, and she blinked, looking over at him as he nodded to her, urging her to remain calm.

She swallowed and nodded, glancing down at her fingers, flinching at the sight of her blood-drenched palms. She balled her fingers into two tight fists and hid them beneath the table.

When she looked up, pulling calm and serenity over her the way she did when she told delegates of her visions, she saw that Athena had not been fooled.

Reaching out, Allegra grabbed hold of Athena's hand. "I promise I will tell you about that too. Add it to your agenda." She grinned and then sat back. "Max, Athena has a good point. There was a time, before Xenia and I were almost killed, when being submerged in water did more than just bring me peace."

Max got to his feet, his massive form almost engulfing the space around them. "Athena is right?"

Allegra nodded. "It must have had some sort of meditative, focusing effect. Submerged in the water, I heard the voices of women, sometimes a few at the same time, at other times just one voice."

"What were they saying?"

"At the time...they were telling me it all depends on me and that I must stay the path. Just hearing those voices terrified me."

"And then, when you thought Neptune was trying to kill you, you stopped immersing yourself in any body of water out of fear?" murmured Athena. "It does seem to me an effective method to ensure you do not access these voices."

"And who do you suppose these voices are?" asked Allegra, merely voicing the question to fill the tense air.

Max sighed. "I can't think of anyone other than the other Oracles of Delphi. Perhaps this is the most natural way to maintain a line of communication among the oracles."

Allegra sucked in a small sob as she shook her head. "It does make sense. I've always been a water baby. Why else would it have been so easy to compete in the Olympic G—"

Athena gasped, then let out a shocked cry. "You're *that* Allegra?"

Wide-eyed, Allegra looked at Athena, aware of Max's wide grin. "You follow the Games?"

Athena nodded. "Who doesn't? Never missed a one. And I was on my feet, yelling your name out so loud the neighbors were banging on the wall to tell me to shut up. I swear I cried when you won. Take that Augustus Poole." Athena slapped her hand on the table, the sound echoing like a gunshot around the cabin. "Bastard thought women couldn't compete against men and win."

Allegra chuckled. "Not that my winning stopped him from continuing to lobby against co-ed races. He went around telling people that Jun Yong Park and Leo Pelham had to slow their speeds in order to *allow* me to win because it would look bad for them if they beat a woman."

Athena's eyes were wide as she shook her head. "I just didn't realize you were *her*. Guess we've never had a Pythia succeed at something other than prophecies before."

Allegra lifted a finger. "Not that we know of."

Sober now, Athena nodded. "Not that we know of…. So I guess now we figure out a way to find out if Neptune is innocent or guilty?"

Allegra lifted an eyebrow. "Exactly. We cannot rule out the possibility that Neptune could possibly see me as a threat and truly wishes to stop me."

Athena's face darkened, her mouth turning upside down. "Sadly, I have to agree. We can't not consider his possible reasons. Although, I would like to state now that I don't believe he would hurt you."

Allegra smiled and patted the surface of the table. "Now that I think about it, I never wanted to believe it either. Let's hope you are right. That's one heartbreak I will gladly live without."

CHAPTER 12

*T*he rest of the flight passed in a calmer silence than Allegra had expected. She knew that Max's anger had not dissipated, the mystery surrounding her possible trip into the future had presented a problem, one that had redirected Max's concentration away from Allegra's veering from the path of safety.

But just because she'd avoided a telling off from Max didn't mean that Allegra was still not worried.

What had the vision meant? And if it wasn't a vision, how was she meant to get her head around such a reality? Yes, she had a birth certificate that claimed her birth date was 100 years in the future, but if that was at all related to her dream, she had to find a way to be certain. There were too many things that hung in the air, too many of those things also bearing large question marks. Had she really seen her mother in the moment she'd made the decision to give Allegra up? And could she even hold it against Jocasta? And further to that, was the other issue that Allegra had not yet touched upon.

Aurelia.

The Pythia that Allegra had never met. But a woman who had

been watching over Allegra from birth. Aurelia had brought Allegra back from the future, had inserted her into a life with a family, who to this day, Allegra had believed to be her birth parents. Allegra stilled for a moment as she considered how she felt with that particular truth facing her head-on. Did she feel any different toward her father and mother knowing they were adopted and not her biological parents? She gave a slight shake of her head. No. Her love for her mother and father was true, and would remain unaffected no matter who her birth mother was.

But, even though she could accept the situation, she was curious as to whether Aleks and Diana Damascus had been at all aware of Allegra's true destiny? And a more urgent question was the glaring coincidence of the fact that Allegra's surname on her birth certificate was the same as her adopted parents.

Then Allegra smiled.

Perhaps Aurelia was smarter than Allegra gave her credit for. Had it been Allegra making the arrangements, she too would likely have selected parents with names that would match as closely to the child's true parentage as possible. Allegra rubbed her forehead and then rested her head back against the reclined seat. She stared out at the clouds in the blue sky, considering her next steps. Perhaps Mara would know something, perhaps Aurelia had more hidden documentation somewhere on the estate, just waiting for her to uncover it when she was ready to know the truth.

Still, even if she were ready, there was still the other matter of how.

How had Allegra been transported to the future, a process that she was certain was not a simple thing? There would have been a summoning, rites performed. Some way to direct the spirit of Aurelia to the future. That left the question of how Allegra had managed to tag along unnoticed.

Leaning her head against the window, Allegra considered Athena's words in favor of Neptune. She supposed that she ought to attempt the use of the pools at the estate, if only to see if her own reaction to water was still the same. Perhaps she'd been reluctant at first to believe Athena's claim that someone else may have been attempting to drive a rift between Allegra and Neptune. But now that she thought about it further, she was able to see the likelihood of the theory.

With thoughts of swimming filling her mind, Allegra fell asleep for the last three hours of the flight, her dreams leading her in an endless looping replay of the visit to Jocasta, her near-death drowning when the *Qurux* sank, and the replay of Cathenna's terrible death at the hands of Langcourt, and then the dreams of blood-stained hands, and of Corina's pale face as she breathed her last breath.

MARA LET out a cackling laugh as she bustled around the table serving Max, Allegra, and Athena their lunch. Les was noticeably absent, and the old woman seemed to take a particular delight in attending to the trio. "Max, my boy. Whatever gave you the impression that Allegra would obey your commands?" the woman asked, snickering as she took a seat and filled her own plate.

Freshly baked chicken filled with herbs, dried fruit, and slices of lemon, whole baked potatoes drizzled with butter, pepper and salt, baby carrots and courgettes from the estate's farm. The meal smelled delicious, and Allegra knew it would taste amazing, but she steeled herself against diving in and waited for Mara to sit back and study the faces around the table.

She stared pointedly at Max, clearly still waiting for an answer.

The commander let out a pained breath, Allegra and Athena both hid their smiles, and Mara's eyebrow rose a fraction higher. She was not a patient woman.

"Common sense," Max said, stabbing a piece of chicken and shoving it almost violently into his mouth. "And a responsibility to the team."

Mara snorted. "I thought you knew the girl well," Mara commented as she too tucked into the meal.

Allegra busied herself with her own plate, attempting to drown out Max's simmering anger with the taste of delicious chicken and the odd burst of sweetness that would hit her tongue when she bit into the dried fruit.

"I thought so too," Max lamented between bites. "Seems I was wrong."

Allegra swallowed and said, "I've already explained. You were already on the water, Athena was back on the ship helping the refugees board. I was the last one to leave. And two girls were still missing. It wasn't like I had a choice. The ship was sinking, I can hold my breath longer than the average person. It made sense to go, and to be quick about it."

"And how did that work out for you? Stuck in a cabin on a sinking ship with only a pocket of air to keep you alive? Sounds to me like things didn't exactly go according to plan."

"But it did go to plan."

Max lifted an eyebrow, his fork hovering half an inch from his potato.

"The two girls were saved," said Allegra simply. Then she focused on her food, determined that be the end of it.

But Mara wasn't having it. "So you disagree with Allegra's decision? You prefer those two girls to have died?"

"That's not what I was saying, old woman. Stop twisting my words."

Mara shrugged. "Seemed to me that it was an either-or situation. Ship is sinking, girls are inside, everyone's gone. Allegra made a decision and saved those girls. Had she waited, they could have died. Or perhaps one of you died too when the ship rolled over."

Max let out a huff. Athena had been oddly silent, and when Allegra glanced over at her, she was surprised to see the woman frowning at Max.

Allegra smiled. So even Athena was seeing the sense in Allegra's defense.

"Max," asked Athena softly, "is there another reason for your...anger with Allegra's decision to go in without telling us?"

Max's eyes narrowed as he stared at the demigod. He would likely have assumed she'd back him up so it made sense he'd be a little affronted. "No. There is no other reason. The Pythia was reckless. She put her life in danger."

"But surely the circumstances would allow for a little leeway in this situation?"

"Leeway?" Max asked leaning forward. "What would you have done had Allegra died in that ship?"

Allegra lifted a finger to point out Xales' uncanny knack for appearing when she most needed him, but Max threw her a dirty glare and she settled back, hiding a smile.

Athena shook her head. "I don't think that would have been an issue," murmured Athena, also sitting back, as though Max's fury was tangible enough to reach out and strike her.

"But what if it was? Do the lives of two people have a greater value than that of the Oracle of Delphi? Would those two girls have been in a position at any point in their future to save thousands and thousands of lives? To avert disasters over and over again, to ensure humanity remains on the correct path?" Athena opened her mouth to reply, but Max shook his head. "I don't believe so. Not unless one of those two girls were the next Pythia. Can you not see that by risking your life, you are also risking the lives of all those hundreds of thousands of people you will save in the future?"

Allegra's jaw hardened. "I know my responsibility, Max."

"But that's just it. It's not at all about responsibility. It's way more than having an obligation to help people. I know you. I know how you feel about the people whose lives you save."

"That's the very reason I went after those girls."

"I understand that. And maybe this time you came away with your life. But what happens if the next time you race off without backup and get yourself in a spot of danger and none of us are there to help? What then? What if you die?"

Allegra shrugged. "If that happens then I believe the world will continue to turn." Allegra knew the words were flippant, but she wasn't sure what else to say. She understood what Max was trying to say. But she stood by her decision to save those girls.

Max was shaking his head as though he was reading her mind. "I can see I'm getting nowhere." Max glanced over at Mara. "You want to help me out here?"

Mara clamped her mouth shut.

"I'm surprised, Mara. I recall you were one of the first people to chastise Aurelia if she ever endangered her life. You never liked her leaving the estate at all. In fact, I remember you telling me off and attempting to get rid of me because Aurelia called to tell me a tsunami was coming but she needed help to figure out exactly where."

Mara grunted. "That was a bit too dangerous. Besides, Aurelia was already seventy-four years old at the time."

"So, what you're saying is that since Allegra is young, it's okay to risk her life?"

Mara didn't reply. She took small bites of chicken and carrots and chewed loudly.

"A young Pythia is just as dead as an old Pythia, no matter what her age. Add in the fact that Allegra is the last of her line, and I'll repeat that in case it wasn't clear...the very last of her line?"

Mara snorted and got to her feet. Plate in hand, she stalked off, pausing on the threshold to look over her shoulder at Max.

"Then perhaps you had better get to work on fixing that situation, hadn't you?" she snapped before flouncing off down the hall.

Allegra's eyes were wide, a smile teasing the corner of her mouth. Athena looked over at her, expression curious and just as reluctant to show her amusement.

Max let out a sigh, although one look at his face confirmed that Mara had hit a sore spot with her comment.

Allegra got to her feet and went to Max. "I'm sorry if I scared you. I didn't think about the consequences. All that mattered to me at the time was saving those two girls, and I didn't consider that I could possibly have died in the process." She let out a sigh, vaguely aware that Athena had left the dining room as Max got to his feet. Looking up into his eyes, she laid her hands on his chest. "I know what you are worried about, but I don't think I have it in me to weigh my own life against two innocent children and truly believe that mine is worth more than theirs."

Max gripped Allegra's hands in his. "And that's what makes you such an exceptional person. It's what I love about you Allegra, that passion you have for each and every living soul. I understand that, I really do. But there will come a point when you will have to make decisions in terms of the good of the many. It may sound callous and cruel, but it's a reality you need to face. If you had died saving those girls, you wouldn't be around to help if tomorrow a tsunami rolls over the Eastern shore of Indus? You wouldn't have been here to predict it, and because of one sudden decision hundreds of thousands of lives are lost."

Allegra let out a sigh and rested her forehead on Max's chest. "Why is all of this so hard? I'm beginning to think I'm not strong enough to keep going with this job and come out the other end with my sanity intact. I wish I could talk to Aurelia...find out how she managed so well."

Max let out a rough laugh. "What makes you think Aurelia was sane?"

Allegra swatted his chest. "Watch what you say. You do not want a Pythia to decide you were worthy of being haunted."

Max let out a shudder. "Apollo save me." Max curled an arm around Allegra's shoulders then gave her a squeeze. "Please, could you check with me in the future before making any rash decision?"

Allegra nodded solemnly.

"Because if you don't, I'll be forced to leave you at home from now onwards."

Allegra gasped. "You would not dare."

"Don't even test me, woman."

The laughter that followed was filled with warmth, affection, and only a touch of fear. Because fear was a constant companion for Allegra. Something she recognized in Max as well. And she was glad she had him there to stand beside her at the worst of times.

They spent the next few minutes discussing what Queen Sonali's plans were for the refugees, and Allegra left the dining room sometime later, happy in the knowledge that she'd saved precious lives. And always saddened to know that weighing lives was something that she'd need to face in the future.

She only hoped that time was a long time coming.

CHAPTER 13

*A*llegra had to admit that Aurelia's choice of area in which to build her estate had been brilliant. The place was remote, secluded, only accessible via helicopter or light plane. The terrain was rugged, making it hard for intruders to access the property, thereby assuring the residents of their security and privacy.

Now, as Allegra walked along a stone path that wended its way along the edge of the lawn that surrounded the main villa, she came to a stop to study the building, to take it all in.

When she thought about her home back in Fornia, Allegra did feel a pull of sadness, that she'd left everything she'd built to come hundreds of miles away, with the prospect of returning seeming more and more unlikely as time went on. She'd been so busy since her trip to Qusqu that even though she desired a short trip home to fetch a few things, to air the villa out, to make sure the pool was in good condition, she'd had to put those plans aside as visions appeared and she'd headed off to far-flung places to figure out how to stop the next impending disaster.

As Allegra headed within the trees, she paused, the thought that she may resent being the Pythia bringing her to a sudden standstill. Did she truly believe her responsibilities to be a burden? She resumed walking, taking the path that would lead her down to the lake, and while she walked, she considered her feelings. Yes, she'd been thrust into this life without any warning or preparation. Yes, she'd resisted; she'd had a different idea of what she'd wanted for her life. But there'd been too many events that had occurred that had helped her to understand her value.

Of course, she'd had her moments where she'd wondered if her only value lay in her prophetic abilities. But those thoughts weren't the ones she'd usually entertain. Of course, she did suffer from the usual bouts of low self-esteem. But she'd never given in to them in the past. Least of all allowing those feelings to take over her life.

Now, though her life had taken a path she'd never considered, she had to think about what this unwanted path had also brought to her. Before she'd seen her first vision, Allegra had been lonely. And alone.

Except for Xenia and her family, that is. The Silanyo's had taken Allegra in after the deaths of her parents, Diana and Aleks Damascus, when she was sixteen. But Xenia and her family had been the only other people in her life who had truly cared for her.

Discarded by her ex for a pretty socialite, overlooked for promotions, ignored by the corporate type who ran her father's business. Now she had a family, as strange as that sounded.

Athena was her closest friend. Incan demigod who shifted into the form of a jaguar, Athena had saved Allegra's life in Qusqu, and she'd joined Max and Allegra when their mission in Peru had been completed. Athena had sworn to remain at Allegra's side, vowing to protect her with her life.

Max, the man who'd served the previous Pythia and who had found Allegra and made her realize what she was. He'd taught her how to access her visions, helped to voice the visions she saw, helped her track the locations down and save so many people. Now he was more than just her guide and friend, their partnership having blossomed slowly into a burning passion. She trusted him more than she'd ever trusted anyone before. That itself had been a pure leap of faith.

And then there was Mara, the grumpy, crotchety, old woman who'd served as Aurelia's handmaiden, a running joke in the compound being the woman was as far from a maiden as was possible to be. Mara doted on Allegra although she was careful to not be too overt. She ensured the meals were to Allegra's liking, that she had clothing and weapons to choose from, that she built her strength and fighting skills along with her visionary skills. The woman was so old that often Allegra would feel a tug of fear in her heart, the awareness that the day would soon come when she'd have to say farewell to Mara.

And then there was Les. Celestra Avesta was still healing from a tragedy that Allegra would not wish on her worst enemy. She'd lost her little boy, murdered by a mafia who had attempted to use Les' access to the ambassador and her links to the NGS government. They'd taken the baby, held him hostage for months, using Les to manipulate agreements and treaties.

But Allegra had seen what was about to happen in Qusqu and had arrived in time to save both Les and the city. But Les was still healing, and Allegra suspected she would take a long time to regain any amount of emotional strength.

As Allegra descended the small incline that would lead her to the lake, she spotted movement, a blonde head bobbing along the shoreline.

Allegra reached the pebble-strewn beach and approached Les who was wading in the water's edge, uncaring the hem of her dress was soaked and clinging to her calves.

Allegra's feet hit the pebbles, and Les looked over her shoulder, a smile breaking out on her face. "You're back," she said, turning toward Allegra as she too approached the water's edge.

"Yes. Back, alive, and well."

"Did you save them? The people you saw in your vision?" Les

asked, her voice still holding a strong amount of awe at Allegra's ability. Considering Allegra had seen Les' tragic death on a vision, the details of her home so specific that even Les could not deny the accuracy.

Allegra nodded. "It was as I suspected. The refugees' bought passage to Indus hopping for a new and better life, but they ended up trapped by slavers, who intended to sell the girls to the highest bidder, and then turn the men and women into slave labor. We got there in time to save them."

Les' forehead scrunched. "We got word that the ship sank?" she asked, worried.

"It sank, and two of the children were trapped inside. I'm in a bit of hot water right now with Max." Allegra laughed and waded into the waves.

"Oh? Why?"

"He's upset because he believes I could have died and that I was being reckless."

Les held onto Allegra's arm. "Back up there. What do you mean could have died?"

Allegra let out a sigh, aware that the look on Les' face meant she wasn't going to get much support. "The ship was sinking. The two girls were trapped in the captain's cabin. Max and Athena had already left the ship, and I was meant to be on the last boat out, but I couldn't leave the girls. And I couldn't get word to Max. So I went in."

"I'm not surprised Max is upset with you. That's extremely reckless." Les' eyes flashed with anger, the most amount of emotion the woman had displayed in months. Allegra wasn't sure if she should be upset or happy that Les was now also mad at her.

"I can hold my breath longer than anyone else. I knew I'd be fine."

"So why was Max angry then?"

"Because I let the girls go but the ship rolled over, and I ended up stuck inside the captain's cabin."

"Oh, this just keeps getting better and better doesn't it?" Les folded her arms. Had her foot not been submerged, Allegra was sure the woman would have been tapping it onto the stones.

"It's not so bad. I had air. I was fine. Then the ship shifted, and I got out. Everyone was fine in the end. No harm done."

"Then why is he mad?"

Allegra groaned. "Because I was underwater for forty minutes, and they were terrified. When I came out, Max was furious."

"He's got every right to be furious. He cares about you more than you know. He must have nearly died of shock thinking you could have died."

Allegra nodded. "I understand that. But I couldn't sacrifice the lives of those girls just because mine would have been in danger. I've already been through this with Max and Athena, I was fine. But I know I was reckless."

CHAPTER 14

*A*llegra watched Les as she walked slowly across the beach, her golden hair shining in the midday sun. The woman walked with sensual grace and sometimes the truth of who Les was to Max hit Allegra hard.

They'd been lovers. Max had even admitted that he'd considered marriage and had Les not become angry and bitter, they would likely have ended up married. The thought didn't upset her as much as she'd expected, although the fact that Max had almost given up his relationship with the Pythia Aurelia to make Les happy, did make Allegra wonder if the woman was pretending when she expressed her loyalty to Allegra.

Still, Les hadn't shown any sign of lying. She'd submitted to Allegra's instructions and guidance, obeyed every instruction to exercise, to learn to fight, to use weapons. Mara hadn't held back, insisting that the only way Les would grow stronger was when she allowed her physical form to become stronger and harder.

And Mara had been right. The longer Les had trained, the stronger she'd become emotionally. Now, Allegra knew she could easily have taken Les along with her if she needed a bodyguard.

But skill was one thing, performance under pressure, something else entirely.

Les still had a ways to go before she could go into combat and come out the other side still whole.

Combat meant there was always a chance you could lose someone you cared about. Allegra's bloodied hands were enough proof of that.

When Les left the beach, disappearing into the trees then emerging up on the hillside track that curved around the hill toward the main house, Allegra turned to face the water. She'd come for one reason only, and now that she was alone she had no reason to delay.

Waves rode the surface of the Qocha Riti, or Lake of the Snow, the glassy darkness broken in a continuous motion, lapping at her ankles as though offering a gentle invitation.

Taking a deep breath, Allegra waded further into the water, moving deeper until the waves slapped against her thighs, and then her hips, and at last encircling her waist.

The water was cool, clear, fed by a waterfall that rose high up in the Andes mountains to the west of the estate. The water in the Qocha Riti was so clear that Allegra could see the multitude of pebbles, every color imaginable, beneath her feet. They prodded and poked the skin beneath her feet, a constant reminder that this was no sandy beach.

A golden fish darted past, wide translucent fins undulating as it disappeared among the rocks. To her left a crab crawled from a hollowed-out stone, its pincers raised as though in defense, before it waddled around and headed off behind a collection of dark rocks.

Surrounded by nature, enveloped by water, Allegra felt a peace filter deep inside her, lifting her mood.

She went further into the lake until the water lapped at her chest, splashing her face when the waves grew stronger. Allegra's long shift dress clung to her body, and she supposed—rather belatedly—that she should have removed it before entering the lake, but she hadn't been thinking of clothing at the time.

She'd felt the magnetic pull of the water, as though the waves had entranced her with their sultry music, and now she almost felt like sobbing as she recognized the depth of the longing she'd suppressed all this time.

Taking a deep breath, Allegra pushed off the lakebed and swam further out, her strong arms and legs pushing her off to a point where the bed of the lake appeared a bit more distant. Still, the water was glassy, and only here and there the scuttling of a crab or a crayfish disturbed the sand.

Soon, Allegra was in the middle of the lake, and she turned in a slow circle, treading water as she moved fluidly around the way a dancer would move to music. Taking a deep breath to fill her lungs, Allegra sank into the lake, reveling in the feel of the water closing over her head, cocooning her in the safety of its liquid embrace.

Sinking lower and lower, Allegra only stopped her descent when her feet touched the stony bed. There she straightened and stared around her, studying the waters that shimmered with iridescent flashes of fish, moved as though alive with the creatures of the waters.

Here Allegra found her peace again, recalling that day inside the pool at home.

She'd felt terror then, voices that called out to her only while beneath the water had scared her.

But she knew so much more now. Now she knew more about who the women were who'd called to her. The voices had not threatened her, and in fact, they'd sought only to comfort her.

A feeling of joy filled Allegra as she let herself fall backward, allowing the water to keep her hovering so far beneath the lake's surface.

As she turned over and over, her hair brushing against her cheeks, Allegra heard the whispers in her mind. The voices returned, their haunting music bringing hot tears to her eyes. Allegra blinked them away, afraid that if the owners of those voices were to materialize beside her, she'd miss them entirely.

The thought sounded far-fetched to her, but if she really thought about it, nothing was really all that far-fetched was it?

Here she was at the bottom of the lake attempting to commune with oracles long dead. Anyone would declare her insane should they know the strange thoughts swimming around inside her head.

Blinking Allegra swam around in an endless circle, listened as hard as she could to the voices. At first, they sounded like a chorus, whispering words that she almost couldn't recognize. But soon she was able to pick a few familiar voices out of the choir.

Jocasta's voice was clear, her young dulcet tones filling Allegra's ears, only she wasn't able to hear the words. It was as though she could hear her calling, but the other voices blurred the words.

The second voice she recognized was that of Cathenna. She was only able to identify the ancient oracle's voice because she'd heard her speak in the visions she'd had. The memories of Cathenna's death made Allegra want to sob, the reality of her familial connection to Cathenna becoming starkly clear.

Allegra swallowed against the throb in her throat and tried to focus on the final voice that was so very familiar.

But no matter how hard she listened to the woman's words, Allegra couldn't put her finger on the identity of that voice.

Still, she forced herself to focus on the voice, to parse the words.

"You have all you need at your fingertips. What you seek you shall find when you are ready to know the truth."

Allegra frowned. "What in Apollo's name did that mean?"

Unsure of how to communicate with the Pythia, Allegra thought the question hoping she would get the question across. "What truth are you talking about?"

The woman laughed, confirming that Allegra had succeeded in projecting her words. "You confuse yourself with too many questions. You muddy the waters. Stop making things so much more difficult. Focus harder on what you need to know, and the answers will come to you."

"Why does everything have to be so cryptic?" Allegra asked. "Who are you?"

The woman laughed again, the sound so familiar it gave Allegra goosebumps. "When you know, you will know."

And then, just like that, the voice was gone, along with the presence of all the other voices, leaving Allegra alone at the bottom of the lake.

Although she felt a little off balance, Allegra had achieved what she'd come to do. She'd communed with the voices, understanding that her fear had been very much misplaced. As she swam toward the shore, she berated herself for being so quick to fear the voices.

How much help had she denied herself by believing the whispered words had meant she was slowly going mad?

CHAPTER 15

*E*merging from the water, Allegra made her way across the pebble beach toward the tree-line, paying no attention to the sodden fabric as it molded itself against her curves. She followed a path through the trees, this one taking her on a longer trail on her return journey, as she hoped to dry off somewhat before she reached the villa.

Sounds in the brush up ahead brought Allegra to a slow stop as she tilted her head and focused on the noises, shutting out the chirping of crickets and tree frogs, and the low hum of bees and wasps.

Not far off from where Allegra now stood, came the hollow thud of hoofbeats pounding the solid earth, and then a snort and a huff peppered the air.

Allegra smiled and headed toward the noise, pushing a giant palm frond aside to see Xales standing in the middle of a small clearing. The great beast tossed his head, the sunlight filtering in through the canopy above glinting off the brass ring in his nostrils. She closed in on him and was about to reach out for his head to pat him—the usual way she greeted him these days— when Xales reared up onto his hind legs, giving Allegra such a fright that she backpedaled, lost her balance and landed hard on her ass.

The throbbing of her injured behind went entirely ignored as Allegra glanced up to stare at the sight of her familiar as he shifted form slowly, his forelegs transforming into human arms, though his hind legs remained those of a giant boar. His skull, eyes, and face shifted and transformed, the large snout shimmering away, the nose turning into something much more human.

Moments later, Allegra stared dumbfounded at the half-man half-boar who stood before her, a smirk on his face.

She'd seen the sculptures of Pan, the mythological half-goat, half-human, and Xales now resembled the cheeky creature, only the boar-man's chest and arm muscles bulged, assuring Allegra that he was still supremely strong, even if his upper body was now that of a fully-grown man.

He bowed low, dark brown hair tracing his shoulders and brushing his cheeks. "I must apologize, my lady. I did not mean to frighten you," he said then straightened, his golden eyes glowing with an intensity that almost elicited a shiver from Allegra.

Allegra's mouth was open, and she slowly became aware that she was still sprawled on the grass. She cleared her throat and boosted herself to her feet, dusting off her damp behind before straightening to meet his gaze. Xales' gaze. "You can transform?" she asked softly, her brow furrowing with confusion even though she was well aware of what she'd just witnessed. She shook her head and scanned him from head to toe before asking, "Why did you not do this before?"

Xales shook his head slowly, his expression darkening. "You were not yet ready," he said, his low baritone reverberating around the clearing.

"And I suppose you now believe I am ready?" she asked dryly, thinking about the cryptic words of the Pythia she'd so recently spoken with. Then Allegra shook her head and let out an exasperated sigh. "I'm talking to a half-man, half-boar."

"How hard is that to process? Athena shifts into a panther," Xales replied, an eyebrow cocked.

"That's different. She's a demigod," Allegra muttered, still unsure how to deal with a talking boar-man.

Xales tilted his head to one side. "And you believe I am not a demigod?" He frowned as though Allegra had claimed something he was finding hard to understand.

"How would I know? I know nothing about you. Remember, you didn't exactly come with a user manual."

Xales chuckled. "My apologies. I shall endeavor to ensure that the next Pythia is availed of the necessary user manuals in order to transition her more comfortably."

"Good for the next Pythia," Allegra muttered as she pulled her dress away from her moist skin. The fabric had dried, but it was still pretty much transparent.

Until now, Allegra wouldn't have thought twice about being naked in front of her familiar. But seeing him on two legs, making intelligent conversion, looking rather like an attractive man, made her uncomfortable.

"It's quite fortunate that you chose this moment to transform," she said. "I've been meaning to thank you for saving my life. I'm certain I would not have survived had you not arrived in time."

"You need protection, my lady. It is my duty to protect you." He tipped his head in a shallow bow.

"Protection? I needed saving," Allegra muttered.

Xales shook his head. "You were well capable of saving yourself, my lady. The help I offered was only in order to keep you safe during your vision."

Allegra squinted at the boar. "You knew about that?"

"I've worked alongside oracles for thousands of years. I understand all too well how you could have reacted once you slipped into the time stream."

Allegra nodded, a little unsure of how to react. Xales had been at her side since the beginning, even before she'd truly accepted that she was the Pythia. He'd scared her at first, but he'd consistently saved her life, over and over again. And she'd grown fond of him.

No. She'd grown fond of a giant, snorting, stomping boar.

Now she was facing a half-human, half-man, and having great difficulty in thinking straight.

Putting a hand to her head, Allegra took a deep breath and said, "I need a moment. Sorry, Xales. It's just…"

"I understand." The boar-man chuckled as he walked over to lean against a nearby tree. "You are not the first Pythia to need time to accept that I'm not just a boar."

Allegra settled onto a grassy patch beneath a tall tree. "So when were you first paired with the Pythia?" Allegra asked, merely to ensure she maintained a connection with him. The last thing she wanted was to end up alienating her familiar. That wouldn't bode well for her future safety.

Xales lifted his eyes to the small patches of blue sky that could be seen from their little spot. "I believe my first charge was the second Pythia, the niece of the very first recognized Pythia. That was over three thousand years ago now."

"Oh? How far down the line was Cathenna?"

Xales tilted his head. "Cathenna was the seventh Pythia, so my sixth charge, some two hundred years after my first Pythia." Xales fell silent, and Allegra wondered if his memories of Cathenna were filled with pain. From her own visions, she had no doubt he'd recall pain more than anything else.

Allegra smiled gently. "From what I can tell she was a lovely person." Then she paused and squinted at Xales. "I suppose there is no guarantee that the Pythia will automatically be a kind soul."

Xales nodded. "That is a keen observation, my lady. But I can confirm that Pythia Cathenna was one of my most wonderful and kind charges. Her heart was filled with love and devotion to her family and to her people." Xales let out a deep sigh.

Allegra glanced over and met his intent gaze. "Very well. I accept you are real and I'm not hallucinating. So, why did you decide to show me your true form now?"

Xales bobbed his head then exhaled what appeared to be a puff of sparkling steam.

A good reminder that the creature is magical, Allegra.

"My responsibility is to keep the Pythia safe. The form that Apollo gave me all those years ago was meant to aid me in ensuring the safety of my charge. Though I have fulfilled my role, at times, a Pythia would reject me, the shock a little too much for her to deal with. The few times that it happened, the relationship was filled with tension, which makes for a very strained life together. Especially as my position at the Pythia's side is a permanent one."

"Who was it that reacted badly?"

"That would be my second Pythia. Her name was Julia, and I'd thought she liked me. I'd revealed myself to her, and she—having been well prepared by my first Pythia Kassandra—appeared to be familiar enough with me. I believe the fault was mine for assuming that her knowledge extended to knowing I can transform into a human form."

"Nobody told her?"

"No. I am still rather miffed in regard to that omission."

Allegra chuckled. "I can imagine what happened, but please, do go on," she said as she waved a hand at Xales who responded with a cheery grin, his affectation almost wolfish.

"I appeared to her in her olive garden, a day or so after a band of thugs had attempted to abduct her from the home of a senator in the north of Greece. I'd believed she'd be in the frame of mind for a reassurance of her safety that went beyond the extent of her own knowledge. I revealed myself in my boar form, as I did with you, and waited as she settled and calmed—she was one of those

Pythias who was startled by most things, including my appearances."

Allegra twisted her lips. In this day and age, with the more modern understanding of human nature, that would have been a sure sign that Pythia Julia would have been even more startled by a half-man half-boar appearing before her.

Xales smirked at the expression on Allegra's face, and she guessed he'd read her well enough. "So I transformed to my human form, ensuring I maintained a comfortable distance from her." Xales paused and let out a weary sigh. "She screamed, turned, and ran."

"Please don't tell me you ran after her?" Allegra asked, her hand over her mouth as she hid a pained grin.

Xales nodded sadly. "I did. In all honesty, I did not believe she would be afraid. I had no concept that a monstrous creature running after her, chasing her between the trees and all the way back to the house would turn her into a squalling, babbling mess."

Allegra could not stop the stunned laugh that escaped her lips. She turned it into a choked cough, but Xales was grinning widely. "I'm sorry, Xales. That must not have been easy for you."

He shook his head. "It was amusing. It still is. The Pythia Julia was quite a...delicate soul."

Allegra shrugged. "I assume not all Pythias are possessed with a strong disposition?"

"No. A fact that I can personally attest to."

"What happened? I mean...did you remain with her?"

"Unfortunately, I am the Pythia's familiar. I had nowhere else to go. Apollo attempted to placate Pythia Julia, but though she calmed down enough to tolerate my boar form, I never believed she was strong enough to stand seeing me in half-human form. I remained in the shadows ever since, appearing only when she needed protection or rescue."

"And of course, that experience made you wary." Allegra smiled sadly, feeling a pull of sympathy for her familiar

"Clearly I was a little dense," he said tapping a finger against his temple.

"Oh no," Allegra whispered, clamping her lips together to avoid smiling.

"It is okay, my lady. It amuses me now too. Although, at the time, I was quite...conflicted. I want to be me. This form is my true physical form, and I longed to find some freedom to roam in my natural body. But any excursions in such a form had to be relegated to the night and to the shadows."

"I thought you were able to roam without the Pythia. You're not tied to me...are you? I hope you're not fixed to where I am all the time," Allegra asked, concerned now at the ramifications of such a situation.

Xales gave a half nod. "Sort of. I am when you are awake. And most definitely if you are in any form of danger or in any situation in which you may encounter danger. But when you are asleep, or in meditation, I take a few moments in which to wander off."

"That's good. But aren't you connected somehow to my mind." Allegra lifted a finger then tapped her temple and pointed to his head. "You know when I'm in danger."

Xales nodded. "Yes. We have a telepathic connection. But past experience has made me all the more wary. There are times when a Pythia may believe she is in no danger and is unfortunately quite mistaken. Even the Pythia is human and fails to have the best judgment of the people around her."

"Ah, I see," Allegra said, her lips twisting in a sad, wry smile. "That makes sense. But it still seems a little unfair. You deserve time off."

The boar-man gave a low chuckle. "Thank you for saying so. You are very much like Pythia Cathenna. That kindness and thoughtful nature." He nodded slowly, his eyes glazing as though he was staring off at a fond memory.

His expression brought a smile to Allegra's face. She, herself had liked Cathenna almost from the first moment she'd seen a vision of the ancient Pythia.

The same ancient Pythia who was Allegra's grandmother.

CHAPTER 16

*A*llegra cleared her throat. "Speaking of Cathenna." Xales snapped his gaze to Allegra's face, his eyes rising in question. "You knew I was in the time-journey. Did you know where I went? I'm assuming you would have a sense of it considering you're meant to protect me..."

Allegra left the question unfinished as she too considered the meaning of her words. Would her familiar also have seen her vision?

As though he'd heard her thoughts, Xales replied, "No. I don't go with the Pythia during such journeys. But I am able to sense your emotions and know if you are in danger. I can't explain it. It makes no sense, but when the Pythias communicate, it's almost unnecessary for me to be in the shared place."

Allegra straightened. "How do you get your head around the fact that when the Pythias join or meet each other, that you, Xales, are with each of them...at the same time?" Allegra shook her head, then pressed her fingers into her temples as though the very idea was enough to explode her brain.

Xales chuckled. "There is a first time for all things. And

believe me, my first time in the joining was supremely confusing."

"Can you sense yourself?"

He nodded. "It is an odd sensation to feel your own mind coming from three places at the same time. I am still attempting to come to terms with it."

"So, when I was underwater, and you were watching over me, you would have sensed who I was with?" she asked carefully, watching Xales' face as he hesitated, as though this was one question he wasn't sure he should answer. Allegra's eyes narrowed as she watched him formulate the best response. Then she held up a hand. "You don't have to answer. I think I know how this can be a problem for you. However you answer, you may be revealing to me something I do not yet know."

He let out a sigh of relief, his shoulders dropping and he smiled. "That is true. If the meeting had been with Pythias of only your past, then it would have been a simple thing to say yes, I know. But a Pythia's own future is often hidden from her prophecies in order to protect both the oracle and the people around her and those she serves."

Allegra nodded. "Because not every Pythia is a good person at her core. It's a sad thing to acknowledge."

"Only the wisest of souls accept a truth regardless of its impact." Xales looked away for a moment then met Allegra's eyes. "There is something more you wish to ask me?"

Allegra glanced away for a brief moment. "It's about Cathenna. Do you know?"

He nodded. "The question is, what exactly do *you* know?" he said, his tone gently. "I wish to clarify in order to ensure I do not reveal a truth you are still unaware of."

Allegra cleared her throat, finding that while she'd listened to Xales' tale, she'd systematically ripped apart a handful of long blades of grass and now her lap was littered with green confetti.

Dusting them off her dress, she said, "I know that Cathenna is my grandmother. I know that she sent her daughters away for their safety because she saw in her visions the danger to each of the Pythia's lives. I know that her daughter Jocasta was sent to the future, and I know that I am her child. And I know that Aurelia brought me to this time period because Jocasta believed I'd be in great danger."

Allegra couldn't bring herself to voice the reason, aware that she'd tucked those facts away in the darkest reaches of her heart, planning to deal with them later. When she was ready.

Xales' baritone drew Allegra out of her thoughts. "Then you do know enough," said Xales as he exhaled deeply. "Have you studied the *Book of Visions?*"

Allegra shook her head.

"The *Codex of the Pythia?*"

Another shake of her head.

Xales cleared his throat, his dissatisfaction filling his tone. "Aurelia kept them in her study," he offered as he watched her face.

He was trying to ascertain if her lack of understanding was by choice. Allegra shook her head. "You know very well I've not entered Aurelia's study."

Xales bowed his head. "That I do. But I'm concerned with whether you even knew about the books in the first place."

"No. There are a few old books in the box in Aurelia's old room. There was Aurelia's own diary but no codex. And two or three small diaries belonging to other Pythias, but nothing bearing those titles."

Xales tipped his head to the side. "The diaries you mentioned, were they more notes rather than large leather-bound books?

"I believe they were. The information was sketchy, and some written in a sort of code I haven't been able to decipher."

"Ah, those would be the notes Aurelia kept on her travels. They do not tell the whole truth. You will need to study the Codices if you want to find out more."

"Thank you Xales. Now that I am aware they exist, I shall find them and begin my reading," Allegra said with a smile.

"It will help you to understand the Pythias of the past. Each Codex is more or less a diary, written by each of the Pythias as a means of transferring knowledge and offering guidance to the next oracle who would take her place."

Allegra grimaced. "Why was I never told about them?"

"No doubt Aurelia would have imparted that knowledge to you had she been alive to train you to become her successor. I must admit, I am surprised that she made no provisions."

"Would Mara have known?"

"Possibly? And should she bear this knowledge, I would then question why they were not given to you earlier."

Allegra lifted an eyebrow. "Have you met Mara?" she asked with a snort. "I think I'll just ask her where they are and leave it at that."

Xales chuckled. "Yes. The woman scares me too."

Allegra laughed at that, the thought of an enormous boar-man cowering in fear before a tiny, wrinkled, old lady tickling her funny bone.

When the laughter subsided, Allegra cleared her throat. "I did find something in Aurelia's box. Evidence of Pythias being hunted and killed by a man named Langcourt. You're familiar with him, given that he had you abducted from Barbarina Town. Someone was investigating suspicious deaths going back a few thousand years. Do you know about that?"

The familiar nodded soberly. "I was given to the Pythias all those years ago mainly because the oracles were sought after, and there were many who wanted to own an oracle for personal gain. The gods were reluctant to intervene but felt some form of protection was warranted. After all, everyone needed the Pythia alive and safe.

"But as the years passed, it became clear that there was a new threat. A specific threat on the life of the Pythia and of every other oracle that followed her. Someone was systematically killing the oracles. At first, it appeared the work of a person who hated the status and power of the oracle. But the threat continued through the centuries, making it clear that it could not be one singular individual. There were considerations given to a secret group of hunters that handed their missions to their progeny. And perhaps that theory bears an element of truth. But soon it became even clearer that the genetic line was also a target. The killers were not only eradicating the oracles, but they were intent on eliminating her descendants too."

"Was there any substantiating evidence to support that theory?" asked Allegra as she considered what she knew about Langcourt.

Xales shook his head. "Much of this is conjecture and supposition. What are your thoughts on the matter, my lady?"

Allegra shook her head. "I'm just thinking it through. We know Langcourt is determined to eliminate me. And his attempts began only when I became the Pythia."

"Which means the Pythias succeeded in keeping you hidden." Xales seemed especially satisfied at that.

Allegra raised a finger in the air. "Which also means Langcourt is working on only what he knows. He has no ability to foresee the future. Which gives us a small advantage over him. He's unable to predict where I will be at any given time, which has made his attempts at assassinating me a reactionary one."

"And Qusqu?" asked Xales, raising an eyebrow.

"What if that was entirely coincidental? Perhaps the gods had arranged for us to cross paths so that I may have kept my promise to Langcourt," Allegra muttered, the urge to punch something sending her fingers curling into fists.

"Your promise?" Xales asked.

"I promised him a most gruesome death as punishment for the horrors he'd visited on so many innocent young children."

Xales rubbed his chin. "And that promise has gone unfulfilled."

"Much to my great displeasure," Allegra said, then let out a sigh. "Again, we lack the means to shed more light on this particular man other than an old photograph of him on safari with what appeared to be his brothers and his father. What do you know about him?"

"My knowledge is limited to what I was told by the oracles I served, and I can confirm that they were always reluctant to provide me with details."

"Sometimes that's more a sign of not wanting to admit to the threat than of their lack of trust in you," said Allegra, well aware of what Xales was thinking.

He dipped his head. "I thank you for saying that, my lady. It appears I know as much as you do about Langcourt. But I do know his name has not been the same through the ages."

Allegra gritted her teeth. "How does a man become immortal? Do you think he had the help of the gods?"

"It is possible. The gods often give gifts to their favored mortals. It would explain why the gods have been reluctant to help or even to advise the Pythias." Then Xales shook his head. "But, I think it unlikely."

Allegra let out a puff of breath, scowling all the while. "Will they help me now? If I ask?" Xales frowned and Allegra clarified, "Do you have a direct line to Apollo?" she asked, smirking.

He let out a hearty laugh. "Not particularly. Apollo has become rather mercurial over the years. He will come if he is needed. Otherwise, I don't believe he's ever responded to a request to meet."

"Always a first time," said Allegra as she got to her feet and dusted her hands together. "So this form…will you walk around the estate this way?" she said, waving her hand at Xales' body.

He chuckled. "I have a glamor that will hide the more animalistic portion of my form. But you need not be troubled. The people on the estate are familiar enough with me. I've lived here for the entire time that Pythia Aurelia has owned the property."

Allegra stiffened as she thought of something. "Does Max know?" asked Allegra, already certain what the answer would be.

"No. Aurelia was adamant we keep it from everyone including Max."

Allegra blinked slowly. Well, that proved Aurelia could be very very wrong.

With a sigh, Allegra headed out of the clearing, calling over her shoulder, "How can I make sure that you have the time to yourself that you need?"

Xales grunted in response. "You would do that?" Then he answered his own question. "Of course you would. You have her ways...."

Allegra smiled as she strolled off, finding herself particularly pleased at the thought that she may be anything at all like her grandmother, the Pythia Cathenna.

ax paced across the tiled floor of the small office which Mara had allocated to him. He'd worked from the spartan room for long hours while Allegra and Athena had trained for weeks on end. Allegra's injuries had healed unusually fast, so Max's fears that she would open her wounds with her excessive physical exertions had been unfounded.

And while Allegra had trained, Max had continued to work, keeping up with the cases his team handled, receiving reports from Marcus Assante, his friend and second in charge at the FAPA head office at the Capitol.

Max had also—much to his dismay—been forced to evade General Aulus' repeated attempts to gain access to Allegra.

And now, as Max paced, he waited for his satellite phone to ring at the appointed time. Aulus had confirmed that he had the president's ear, and no matter what Max's opinion was of the leader of the NGS, compliance was the only option.

Or at least the appearance of compliance.

The phone rang, the shrill noise echoing around the small space. Outside the patio doors—the only thing that was halfway pleasant about the room—a pair of doves took flight, the sound sending them fleeing.

Max shook his head and answered the call.

"Commander Vissarion? Greetings to you," came Aulus' voice, scratchy and tinny over the satellite connection.

"Greetings, General," Max replied, keeping his tone formal and respectful. "How may I help you?"

Aulus let out a laugh. "Young man, who will have to allow me access to the Pythia at some point, I hope you know that. I'm quite certain there is something in your constant refusal that could be seen as breaking the tenets of the Treaty of the Pythia." The man spoke with laughter in his voice, but his words were accompanied by more than a hint of iron.

"I assure you, sir. No tenet is being broken. I am, of course, the NGS delegate to the Pythia. And I am only relaying her wishes. She will let you know if any of her visions affect the well-being of the NGS in any way."

Aulus' grunt came through over the satellite line sounding more as though the man was choking. "I do believe the Pythia is not too busy to personally attend to the retrieval of refugees from a sinking slave ship in Mranma halfway across the world from Argentina, so I don't see any reason for her denial for an audience. Perhaps you could tell her that the president wished to meet with her in person."

Max raised his eyebrows at that. "He wants a personal meeting?"

"Yes, he does. But of course, he will visit with a delegation."

Max grinned, thinking of the last time general Aulus arrived at the estate with an unwelcome delegation. They'd been summarily dismissed by a coldly furious Pythia Aurelia.

Max chuckled. "Sir, I think you will find that this Pythia is not that much different to Pythia Aurelia in her requests."

The silence that followed confirmed that perhaps Max had overstepped in mentioning the embarrassing incident to Aulus.

"At any rate, sir," Max kept talking, "the Pythia has assured me that she will make time for the president. I will have to get back to you with the dates she will see you."

"Dates?" asked Aulus, his voice rising.

"Yes, sir. The Pythia is arranging a summit and is opening her calendar to personal visits from dignitaries around the world. She'll be only too glad to set aside the time to sit down with the president and address his question."

"I see," Aulus replied coldly.

Max smirked. For some reason—purely perhaps because Allegra had been born on NGS soil—the president, the Senate, and every other legal representative of the country, seemed to believe they held a larger stake in the Pythia than any other country of the world.

No. It wasn't Allegra they wanted. The president and his senators wanted access to Allegra's visions. And perhaps having Max as the most senior delegate to the Pythia had also allowed them to believe they held a higher stake in her.

The problem was, Max had spent years working for the government and was familiar enough with their motivations. And while he didn't know the true reasons behind Aulus' and the president's sudden desire to meet Allegra, Max was well schooled in the way the political wheel turned and was experienced enough to hazard a guess as to the reasons behind them. Max had found it exceedingly difficult to identify one among them who acted for the good of anything other than lining his pockets and acquiring more power.

And General Aulus was well aware that Max did not play his game, political or otherwise.

It was a wonder as to why Max still retained his position within the government. But it made perfect sense. The Senate believed Max was their key to the Pythia, so they tolerated his opposition. Which undoubtedly infuriated them to no end each time Max had to turn them down on her behalf.

"Very well, Vissarion. I shall await your confirmation of a date."

The satellite phone emitted a sharp click and Max stared at the receiver. Aulus had cut the call without another word. Max shook his head then tossed the phone onto the desk.

He walked over to the small patio and stood in the small patch of sunshine, soaking up the rays as he tilted his face to the sun. Things had been moving at breakneck speed these last few weeks and Max needed a breather. Allegra probably needed one too.

And, there was also the matter of Langcourt's movements. Max was attempting to ignore the surveillance details and search reports of the man's activities since his departure from Peru.

Though he'd said nothing to Allegra, Max had maintained an open and busy investigation on the man's movements and had tracked him all across the world until he'd lost him only two weeks ago.

The lord was slippery, and he seemed to know all of Max's moves, to a point that Max had considered that he'd had a mole placed inside FAPA or the NGS.

And, given that Langcourt was centuries old, he'd no doubt have amassed an extensive network of illicit contacts. But Langcourt had no idea what kind of adversary Max could be.

Max wasn't about to let the killer harm Allegra. He'd kill the man with his bare hands before he allowed that to happen.

CHAPTER 18

*S*parring with Xales was an unusual experience for Allegra; the sight of the half-man half-boar swinging a heavy sword with ease and skill was enough to make her lose her concentration.

Which she did at various points in the past hour of their training session.

At last, when her frustration had built to a level that she felt anger beginning to filter through, Allegra gritted her teeth and charged, seeing only her familiar's grinning smile.

Their swords struck hard, the sound high-pitched and sharp enough to jar Allegra's ears, the impact sending strong vibrations through her bones.

Allegra sucked in a sharp breath at the odd pain in her inner ear. And that inhalation, accompanied by the sound still ringing in her ears, sent Allegra slumping toward the ground.

As hard as she tried to remain conscious, Allegra couldn't hold on any more than she could have held onto a puff of smoke. Blackness filled her sight, and she didn't even feel it when her body hit the ground.

ALLEGRA BLINKED SLOWLY, *her eyelids unnaturally heavy, and she forced herself to open her eyes. Around her should have been the sparring ground, and Xales with his sword in hand, probably staring down at her in amusement.*

But instead, Allegra saw undulating grassy hills, low buildings lining stone-paved streets and then plumes of smoke and ash in the distance.

Allegra squinted and sat up, a little wary about passing out again. When the world around her didn't spin, she pushed to her feet, knowing almost instantly that what she was seeing was a vision.

Her ears no longer rang with the sounds of the clashing of swords, and she felt completely in control of herself. The only problem was the utter mayhem that surrounded her.

The streets across from her overflowed with cars, the stalled traffic bumper to bumper all the way into the distance. The caravan of vehicles idled, filling the street with exhaust fumes and noise, and only adding to the smoke and ash showering down onto the city.

Long lines of foot traffic snaked away from the hilltop, and from where Allegra stood they looked like nothing more than ants as they flowed down the mountain and away from their homes.

Allegra tore her gaze away from the escaping residents and spun around to scan the part of the city around her, a little shocked to see that she recognized the place. She'd visited Pompeii once, when she was still a teenager, having joined Xenia and her parents on a trip there on summer vacation.

Their dour tour guide had shown Xenia and Allegra around the city, identifying the locations of the earthquake-meters buried deep within the earth. Research stations around the world constantly monitored ground activity sending alerts to the city's councilors who in term notified businesses and institutions around the city.

The people had grown used to being immediately moveable, with a bag prepared for departure in an instant. All valuables were kept in secure heat-resistant boxes within their homes, and residents of the city were trained from a young age to identify the dangers early and how to react in case of an eruption.

Allegra had left the city somewhat disturbed, unable to understand how an entire city of people was happy to remain in such a dangerous environment, and then too, to live lives constantly on edge, waiting for the next disaster to happen.

Now as Allegra stared up at Mt Vesuvius and watched plumes of smoke and bursts of flame flung from the mouth of the volcano, she shook her head and studied the cars and the people around her. How can she identify when this was going to happen?

Allegra hurried along the path, hoping she'd come across a newspaper stand that would give her a date.

But as she stepped forward the scene around her changed, and she was standing again in a most familiar street.

Across from her was Khan's Koffee and up the street was her favorite bakery. Allegra's heart twisted as fear ripped through her. For a moment she froze, terrified of what she was about to see.

And then she took a breath and forced herself to remain calm. Whatever she saw could be averted if she learned as much as she could from what was around her.

Allegra hurried along the street, instinctively avoiding people who were running in both directions, clearly afraid and fleeing.

Beyond the hospital, Allegra could see the hillside where a number of residential communities had been built. But not much remained of them. The mountain was in ruins, the ground split apart with everyone that had once been on the hill now gone, leaving a gaping hole.

A woman was crying in the distance, staring up at the destruction, tears streaming from her eyes as a couple tried to comfort her.

Allegra felt tears burn the back of her eyes, but again she forced herself to focus. She spun around and raced to the coffee shop in search of the weekly specials. The owner often included the date of the Monday.

Skidding to a stop outside the store, she found the place locked up tight, everything inside left as it was before the alarm would have gone off. Tables were strewn with half-eaten sandwiches and mugs of unfinished coffee.

Leaning as close to the window as she could, Allegra squinted at the counter toward the back of the coffee shop and found what she was looking for.

The date on the specials board was two weeks from today, and Allegra filed it in her mind, hope rising within her that she and Max could help do something to stop this destruction.

Heaving a sigh of relief, though still a little concerned that she hadn't awaked from the vision considering she now had the information she needed, Allegra stepped away from the window.

As she turned to survey the small town, she found the view before her shifting to one Allegra was unable to identify.

She was standing within a small market, amidst a screaming mob as people streamed toward the hills. The stalls around her had been tossed aside, as though an earthquake had shaken everything so hard that tables and display walls had all fallen apart.

A rush of sounds behind her had Allegra spinning around in time to see a long caravan of military Jeeps transporting people away at top speed. Everywhere, people and cars streamed away from the shoreline that sat slightly below where Allegra stood.

Her jaw dropped at the sight of the bare sand. Where the beach with its tumultuous waves should have been was now bare sand littered with rocks and dead fish, all the way out almost to the horizon.

And in the distance an enormous wave rose, so high that even from where Allegra now stood it appeared to be tall enough to engulf her entirely.

A resort vehicle raced past Allegra, and she caught sight of a golden emblem, a Balinese dancer, her jewels, and headdress glittered in the sunlight.

The dark man in the Jeep shouted, "Faster, you have to get me out of here." His driver didn't reply although the vehicle did seem to increase in speed. As the Jeep disappeared, Allegra frowned. She knew that man. He was an actor, one she remembered had been cast in the *lead role in a retelling of Helen of Troy. He'd played the part of Menelaus, the cuckolded husband, and had received accolades for his performance.*

Pedro de la Corta.

That was his name, Allegra was certain.

And now as Pedro's Jeep disappeared up the mountainside, Allegra took a breath and studied the surrounding roads and buildings in the distance, private holiday resorts with beach access to each room.

And all those buildings would soon be engulfed in water. Allegra stilled as she watched the tsunami reach the shoreline, starkly aware that there were still hundreds of people attempting to flee on foot who were not going to make it.

And there was nothing she could do about it. Not yet anyway.

And then the wave swept over Allegra, and she let out a low scream, reaching out to grab onto something, anything.

ALLEGRA'S HANDS hit a warm body, and she blinked, opening her eyes to find both Max and Xales beside her. She found her fist embedded in Max's gut, but he appeared to have not noticed, or cared.

"Allegra? Are you all right?" he asked, his tone low as he studied her face. Then he paused and nodded. "A vision?" he asked, already grabbing the notebook he kept in his pocket at all times.

His pen hovered over the paper as he waited for her to catch her breath. She shook her head, still confused. "It was a vision, but it was nothing like my normal visions. It was like I was seeing three visions at once. All happening almost at the same time."

Max frowned as he wrote down her words without asking her anything further.

Allegra sighed and gave him the details of each location, and the timeframe that she'd managed to identify for Fornia. "I couldn't find anything to let me know when the eruption will happen in Pompeii. But for Bali, I think I recognized one of the tourists."

"That's a good place to start," murmured Xales.

Max flicked Xales a sharp look, reminding Allegra that she needed to introduce the pair.

"Who was this tourist?" asked Max.

"Pedro de la Corta," Allegra replied. "He was taken up into the hills so I do think he may survive the tsunami, but I think we can use his presence there to find out when his booking is for. I saw the emblem for the hotel on the side of the car, so we have something to go on."

"But only for Bali and Fornia," Max said almost to himself. "But if these visions happened at the same time, perhaps we are looking at three events that occur simultaneously."

"We'll know as soon as we can place Pedro in Bali. If the dates match Fornia, then we can assume Pompeii will happen at the same time. The only problem is how are we supposed to investigate three simultaneous events. I can't be in three places at the same time."

Even as Allegra spoke the words, she knew they were not entirely true. Still, moving through time was probably not the best solution for their current dilemma.

"Then we split up. We have enough team members, and I can get Marcus to come out with a small team as well." Max closed his notebook and reached for Allegra's arm.

As she got to her feet, Allegra met Max's eyes. "Split up? Are you sure you'll be able to handle not being at my side all the time?" she asked with a smirk.

Max's eyes narrowed. "Where you go, I go. So that's not even up for debate."

Allegra shook her head then dusted off her hands. "It doesn't make sense for you to waste manpower by staying with me. You and Marcus both head a team, and leave Athena with me. She's more than capable of running her own mission. And besides, I also have Xales."

Max let out a soft laugh. "I agree with Athena as a valuable asset. But Xales? He only appears when your life is in danger. What if he's too late this time."

"He won't be too late," Allegra said, a smile blossoming across her face as she turned to look at Xales who gave an almost imperceptible nod.

When Allegra turned back to Max, his expression was a mix of confusion and irritation. "You're very confident about that. But I wouldn't rely on him. It's not as if he can come when you call him."

Allegra laughed softly then waved a hand between Xales and Max. "Max, meet Xales. Xales, meet Max."

The look on Max's face was priceless.

CHAPTER 19

*I*n the following days after the dream, Allegra forced Mara to show her Aurelia's library. Now she stood within the old Pythia's inner sanctum wondering why Mara had been so reluctant to allow Allegra entry to what technically now belonged to her.

Allegra stared at the piles of ancient books now lying all over the tiled floor at her feet. She was seated on a fat cushion, with many of the books opened and abandoned around her.

She found historical accounts of many different Pythias through the ages, discussions on the influences of the Oracles' visions and how it shaped modern history, even a selection of theses claiming the oracles to be overly influential and far too powerful, and suggesting the removal of the Pythia's influence over governments.

Allegra let out a low grunt and boosted herself onto her feet. She stretched and twisted, aware she'd been sitting on the floor for hours now. She hated not having access to the web anymore, and had requested a computer, to which Max had replied that they would need a satellite connection as Argentina didn't have the infrastructure as yet to facilitate access to the web.

Allegra sighed, then downed the remainder of the weak red wine the estate produced, and focused again on the bookshelves. She paused to consider that perhaps Aurelia would have hidden the books that Xales had mentioned and that maybe even Mara had little idea as to their true value.

Walking the length of the room, Allegra studied the walls, searching for a secret doorway, or a false panel, something that could hide the existence of a hiding place.

And Allegra found nothing.

Frustrated, she studying the size of the room, then tapped her lip as an idea popped into her head.

Reinvigorated by her hunch, Allegra hurried to the door to the meeting room outside, the hall where Aurelia would often receive dignitaries and other guests.

Here again, she studied the hall but came up with nothing. Disappointed, she returned to Aurelia's study and stared outside at the small patio area. A wooden pergola offered some shade from the harsh sunlight, assisted by the grapevines weaving their way along the wooden beams.

Allegra stepped outside and turned to study the villa again, her attention shifting to the room beside the study—which had turned out to be Aurelia's, now Allegra's bedroom. Allegra walked the narrow pathway and entered her room through the patio doors then studied the space again.

And she found what she had suspected.

There was a space a quarter of the size of Allegra's study, hidden between the two rooms. Smiling, Allegra returned to the study and concentrated on the wall behind Aurelia's desk again, certain now that something hid a secret doorway.

And then Allegra grinned.

Placing her palm flat on the wall, she began to press hard, tracking along the length of the wall around shoulder height. And, right beside a framed painting of a woman and her three daughters, the wall clicked, and a secret door opened toward Allegra.

She sighed and stilled her racing heart, at the same time inhaling the smell of old paper and dried ink, as well as years of dust.

She'd found the room, and her stomach twisted with nerves at what lay beyond the secret door. Then, taking another deep breath. Allegra entered the room and pulled the door shut behind her.

Inside, the space was dark, although light filtered in through holes in the ceiling, as though channeled in from the rooftop. Dozens of candles were strewn around the room, likely used during Aurelia's nighttime rendezvous within this inner sanctum.

One narrow wall bore a floor-to-ceiling shelf, the opposite a large writing desk on which sat a parchment held open with four shards of crystals. Aurelia had evidently been in the process of writing something, and she'd died before completing the task, proving once and for all that Mara had known nothing about the secret room.

Now Allegra leaned over the paper and studied Aurelia's records.

It had broken my heart to take the child from her mother's arms. Jocasta will never know the pain I felt in separating a mother from her child. Too few know how deeply that act hurts, as only a mother can know what it feels like to be separated from her child.

I feel for Jocasta as I fear she will never recover from the pain of this separation, and I am most afraid that her pain will influence her ability to survive her terrible disease.

I am determined to find a way to tell Jocasta what she needs to know about her child. I was at a loss as to how to ensure she received these messages but I have at last devised a plan. I pray it works to give Jocasta the strength and hope that will help her pull through and survive because I wish beyond anything else that I can reunite mother and child at some point.

Perhaps the idea is somewhat grandiose or fantastical, but I see no reason why I shouldn't assure Jocasta that her decision had indeed been the correct one. How could she have known that I would have no living heirs nor have any knowledge of another surviving Pythia able to take over from me?

A reason enough for me to help Jocasta remain at peace.

ALLEGRA STRAIGHTENED, her heart thrumming loudly as she considered the contents of the letter. This was Aurelia's diary. Was this what Xales had meant? A book filled with the private accounts of all the Pythias through history?

Allegra turned to examine the bookshelf, pulling the first book from the topmost shelf. Turning it over, she stared stunned at the name written on the faded leather cover.

Phemonoe.

From what Allegra had read in her brief research of the Pythias, Sybil was the first Oracle, the oracle who was the progenitor of all the daughters of Delphi.

And Allegra was looking at the writings of Phemonoe. She stood there in shock for a moment, unsure how to process the thought, to accept what she was looking at.

Letting out a slow breath, Allegra carried the leather-bound book to the table, then carefully set aside Aurelia's parchment before laying Phemonoe's book down gently.

Her hands shook, so afraid was she that she would damage the leather, or even the pages. Holding her breath, Allegra opened the cover carefully, and read the inscription on the first page.

Written in ancient Greek, the words of the first oracle seemed to resonate from the pages. From the condition of the paper, Allegra guessed that this was not the true original writings of the

Phemonoe who lived in a time when words were more often carved into stone tablets.

Still, the sense of awe remained, probably because the recordings themselves must have been at least three thousand years old.

Allegra was about to settle into the chair, her thoughts focused on the words of an ancient oracle, when the sound of Max's voice echoed through into the room.

"Allegra? We've found something," Max said from her study.

For the briefest moment, Allegra found herself hesitating, a flash of the question filtering through her mind, *Should I show this to anyone, even Max?*

Was she really mistrusting Max?

CHAPTER 20

*A*llegra shook her head.

She was only in this new life because of Max. Max's connection to the New Germanic States, General Aulus and everyone else who wanted to control Allegra, was her only point of discomfort. But she also knew that Max was entirely loyal to her, and more importantly, to the Pythia—whoever she may be.

She gave a short nod and headed to the secret door. She pushed it ajar and stepped into the room just as Max turned to leave.

"Max?" Allegra called out.

Max stopped in his tracks then spun on his heel, his gaze going immediately to the open patio doors. Frowning, he scanned the room, his expression a little surprised to see Allegra standing near the back wall behind her desk.

"Where—" he began, but Allegra lifted a hand and beckoned him to her.

Without a word, he crossed the study, and when he drew to her side, she pulled the secret door open and waved him inside.

Max's expression remained stunned as he entered the small space and studied the shelf and then the open book on the desk.

"I had no idea this was here," he murmured as he traced a finger along the spines of the dozens and dozens of books. He looked over his shoulder. "When did you find this place?" he asked, a dazed smile curving his lips.

"About an hour ago, I think? Could be longer considering how fascinating this place is. I daresay I lost a bit of time just standing and staring at that shelf."

Max's head bobbed, and then he took a step away. "You can't tell anyone about this place," he said, his voice hard and stern. "You should not have told me."

Allegra blinked at the rebuke and took a short step back. "Why? I trust you, Max. What reason would I have to keep this from you?"

Max's jaw tightened. "Because Aurelia never mentioned this place to me, and I've been with her for decades. To me, that means this repository is meant to be kept top secret, for its own safety, I imagine."

A weary sigh escaped Allegra's lips. "All this secrecy is very tiring. How am I supposed to live knowing I should not be trusting anyone, even those I love?" she asked, her voice quavering.

Max blinked at the words, likely due to her mention of love, but he didn't follow through. Instead, he came toward her, holding her arms. "No matter what, every single person around you, including you, can betray the position of the Pythia. We are all vulnerable." He looked around the room. "I suppose that was the reason Aurelia would have kept this place a secret. I'm positive Mara has no idea it's here either."

Allegra nodded. "She kept the study under lock and key until I demanded to see it. So...it's possible she knew and was attempting to protect it?"

Max let Allegra go and studied the room, its walls and ceiling and then the floor. "It could be possible. This room is a fire-safe." When Allegra frowned at the word, Max continued, "It's standard governmental issue for storing important documentation. All originals are kept in a room constructed out of fire-resistant materials, in this case, stone. And some metal."

"Metal?"

"Yes, in the mortar. It helps prevent a fire from crystallizing the sand in the mortar mix. When sand crystallizes, the movement of air can dislodge the mortar and allow the flames to gain access to the room. Aurelia commissioned the best fire-safe money can buy."

Allegra folded her arms, lifting an eyebrow as she said, "Wouldn't that mean the person who built it would know it's here, and that it contained supremely important documents given that it was the Pythia who commissioned it?"

Max grinned. "Well, that's a mystery for another day, my lady. For now, I have news on our investigation," Max said as he cracked open the safe door and entered the empty study.

Allegra followed and quickly closed the door behind her, more aware now of the necessity to keep the room secret. She went to her desk and sat on Aurelia's battered leather office chair, waiting as Max took a seat in a low-backed stone chair covered in brightly-patterned cushions.

He looked uncomfortable as he wriggled on the soft seat, but Allegra held back her amusement as he took a breath and said, "We managed to track down Pedro. He's currently filming a movie in Reykjavik and has booked a week in an exclusive resort in Bali in order to warm up after the frigid climes of Snæland."

Grinning, Allegra leaned forward, elbows on the desk. "How did you manage to obtain that information? I thought actors of Pedro's status had strict rules about privacy."

Max quirked an eyebrow. "I may have mentioned that the Pythia was interested in arranging a meeting, and I may have dropped a date that fell in line with the one on the baker's board," he said with a mischievous smirk, "and I may have implied that the Pythia would consider meeting Pedro depending on if her itinerary intersects with his during that time period."

Allegra let out a giggle. "So sneaky. Is that what FAPA is all about? Subterfuge and white lies," she asked, laughing softly.

Max winked. "Means to an end, my lady." After a moment of shared chuckles, Max leaned toward the desk. "We now have a confirmed date: seventeen Quintilis. That is only ten days from now."

Allegra got to her feet. "So, what about Pompeii? Do we have anything to go on?"

"Nothing that I was able to find out with my investigative skills. But then again, I didn't expect to. Earthquake and volcanic activity measurements are tricky...best left to the professionals." Max rubbed his forehead, making it clear that the investigation had proven far more taxing than anything they'd encountered to date. He cleared his throat and straightened, dropping his hand as he said, "I've made contact with the geologists and warned them to be on the lookout for activity in those three areas. I'm just concerned about the fact that we have to split up the teams."

Allegra shook her head and sat back down. "Max, what is there to discuss?" she asked, preparing herself for a fight. "I can manage without you. I'm sure we can split the teams in a way that you can be comfortable with. Besides, you have met Xales. He's entirely capable of protecting me in whatever form he chooses to manifest."

Max let out a long breath and fell against the backrest of his seat. "Now that I did not see coming," he said, shaking his head.

"You had no idea? Did you not see him around?"

Max shrugged. "I did, mostly on the estate. But he never told me who he was. I mean, I met him in boar form, yes, but he never came up to me and said 'Greetings, Max. I'm Xales, you know, the four-legged, familiar of the Pythia.'"

Allegra chuckled. "Are you upset that you were not told?"

"A little I think. I was with Aurelia for years, and she never mentioned his ability to take human form either."

"Perhaps another small detail that is best kept close to the Pythia's chest?" suggested Allegra, tilting her head as she studied Max's face. He didn't seem convinced. "Very well then, what is the problem? What do you see is the issue here?"

Max raised his eyebrows. "Nothing in particular. I just would have been happier knowing who he is. And he's...rather large even in human form. He could be dangerous when sparring."

"Max, he's not that much larger than you. And he's been tasked with protecting the Pythias by Apollo himself. I hardly think he's going to get careless and kill one of us. He'd be in pretty deep trouble if that had to happen." Allegra paused, and her eyes narrowed. "Although I'm beginning to wonder if it's not the fact that he can transform as it is what he transforms into. He's pretty nice to look at, isn't he?" asked Allegra, attempting and failing to hide her smile.

Max's jaw tightened. "I suppose he is."

Allegra burst out laughing, "Max, I do believe you are jealous," she said, as she got to her feet and walked around the desk toward Max. She hovered over him, hands on either side of his, gripping the armrest. "You think that I may actually be impressed with Xales in human form. That I like the look of his bulging muscles glistening with perspiration," Allegra raised her hands, cupping them as she said, "the taut shape of his—"

She let out a low squeal as Max grabbed her by the waist and tugged her onto his lap.

"Woman, I do not need to know about Xales' taut shapes."

Allegra was still laughing as she settled on Max's lap, enjoying the closeness. "Admit it. You're jealous."

Max started to shake his head, but Allegra placed a finger on his cheek. "Well, perhaps a tiny bit."

Allegra grinned and shook her head. "Want to know a secret?" she whispered in his ear.

"As long as it does not include you fantasizing about the man naked," Max muttered.

"Xales' human form isn't fully human. He uses a glamor to hide the fact that his lower half is still that of a boar."

Max's eyebrows hit his hairline. "What? Are you serious?"

Allegra nodded. "He appeared in boar form and then transformed into something in between. His upper half is fully human though."

Max smirked. "And the lower half is fully that of a boar?" he asked, squinting at Allegra as she nodded. Then he cupped his free hand giving a suggestive wink, "and his mmh...a boar's as well? Size?" Max let out a low cry as Allegra smacked him hard on the biceps.

"Shut up, Max."

He gave her an innocent look. "I was just curious. I mean, you saw him with your own two eyes."

Allegra pursed her lips. "Well, if you must know, I didn't look."

"Not even a tiny little peek?" Max nudged her arm.

"Not even a tiny peek." Allegra lifted a brow. "I think perhaps I have a regular enough dose of the...uh," she mimicked Max's cupped hand, giving him a sultry stare, "to keep me happy."

Max let out a bark of laughter that filled the study. His chest shook, and Allegra grinned back, enjoying the small respite in which nothing else mattered other than her and the man she adored.

That same man shifted and wrapped his arms around her as he got to his feet. "Perhaps you could do with another...dose? I'll be more than happy to comply should the Pythia wish to sample the...uh..."

Max ignored Allegra as she slapped his chest. He carried her out of the study, and past the meeting rooms, heading toward their bedroom.

Allegra supposed she should have resisted, given that it was still the middle of the day. But she didn't particularly care. Being in Max's arms made up for so much of the misery that she so often found herself immersed in, and the few moments in which she spent enveloped in affection and passion, in the arms of a man with a heart of gold, was well worth the talk that a midday rendezvous would generate.

Max entered their bedroom, shut the door with his foot and tossed Allegra in the middle of the bed.

Allegra lay back on her elbows, offering him a sultry smile, only too ready for her midday rendezvous.

CHAPTER 21

*A*nd they'd reached the end of that journey, celebrating success on the deck of their ship as they watched the pale shores of the city of Atlantis rise in the distance as though emerging from the middle of the ocean.

The wind gusted around Allegra, tugging at the fabric around her legs, pulling hard at her hair and thrusting her long locks into her face. Allegra brushed them aside impatiently, anxious that she would miss the approach to the great city.

But the journey was slow and long enough as the captain maneuvered his vessel along the waters, taking extra care to avoid the sandbanks that seemed to appear without warning. The captain had labeled the waters in this part of the ocean as capricious, but Allegra thought the word too mild. Her visions had told her what horrors would have awaited them had the residents of this city still occupied it. But her visions had told her otherwise. Months ago, the residents had fled, and her visions had been filled with the fear of the inhabitants. The most frustrating aspect of it was that the fears of the people had seemed unfounded and nowhere in her visions had she seen a reason for the people to flee the city.

As the ship drew closer, Goran came to stand beside her, taking deep lungfuls of air as though he wanted to inhale the very reality of the city's existence. She knew she'd only told him what she'd seen because she'd loved his passion for history and archeology, his devotion to understanding the peoples of the past.

Many people, her family, the senate, and even his own friends, had accused him of living with his head in the clouds, of not grounding himself in reality and thereby shirking his role as the husband of the Pythia. Their relationship had blossomed before the weight of being the Pythia had fallen upon her shoulders. Neither she nor Goran had ever expected, or even wanted, such responsibility. And yet they'd both shared that burden and had carried themselves accordingly.

Allegra had shrugged off the criticism as the accusations of the envious, of those who coveted what her husband had. She'd had many suitors, a long line of men who thought themselves deserving of a place at her side. Little did they know that they had all failed the most important test, that should she see their future when she touched them, that very vision no matter what its content, would forever preclude them from ever sharing her life or even her bed.

But Goran had been immune, and being with him was a pleasure in more ways than those of being man and wife. To hug or hold someone, to pass a bowl of fruit, or share a grapple for a ball, all things the normal person could not ever understand. Goran was her island of peace, and she'd go to her death forever grateful for having found him.

And as a woman who knew the worth of the man she loved, how could she ever have passed up the chance to gift him with something he'd dreamed of for most of his life.

But the closer they now drew, the worse she felt. Her stomach twinged, mild pulses of pain at first and then growing worse every second until she couldn't decide if she wanted to vomit or curl up in a ball and cry her eyes out. Something was terribly wrong, and it was directly related to her husband, but she couldn't see it even if she wanted to, because Goran was Immunis.

A blessing and a curse it seemed.

CHAPTER 22

A flock of white gulls swarmed in the air above the ship, diving low and swooning upward to ride the air currents, their screaming, keening cry making the approach to the abandoned city all the more mournful. Another hour went by before the ship finally reached a dock where the entire pier was made of carved marble, and the steps glistened with streaks of gold.

Behind her, the captain let out a low whistle as he stared up at the plinths of the temples in the distance. From their approach, the city had appeared to be circular in construction, and the docks were located along the outer edge of the largest circle which seemed to also act as a barrier against the tide.

A barrier that appeared to have been destroyed in many places.

Goran leaned toward her. "What do you suppose caused that destruction?" he asked, his tone playful.

With a sigh, she said, "A weapon perhaps? Some type of small cannon?" she suggested, glancing at him for a brief moment before shifting her attention back out to the buildings above the docks.

He was silent for so long that she glanced back at him, concerned that perhaps he was angered by her suggestion. But Goran's smile had only fallen for a moment and then his eyes lit with amusement. "Beautiful and smart. I quite like it," he said seductively.

He'd always loved the fact that she was intelligent, that she could speak her own mind. But now, Allegra didn't have the heart to reveal that she'd seen it in her vision when she'd first learned of the existence of this fabled city.

Fat cannons spewing fireballs, sending them smashing into the pristine white marble walls of the docks. She only hoped that the rest of the city had escaped the destruction.

The crew left the ship moored at the docks and proceeded to explore the city. Armed in case they encountered a dangerous element, they spread out around the circular islands, finding many a sight to exclaim over. But Goran bore a single-minded determination as he hurried along marble streets edged in gold and silver, walls covered in mosaic paintings so lifelike that the only thing that made them unusual was that they had been created with chips of precious metals instead of paint.

Allegra had found herself quite entranced and had ignored Goran's summons more than once. The images painted onto walls and floors pulled her closer, and she could have sworn she'd heard a low hiss of whispers the closer she got. Only when Goran's call had borne a hint of annoyance did she stir from her trance to hurry over to him.

He was standing in the center of the smallest of twelve circles. At the very center was a miniature temple of Neptune, tall enough for a full-grown man to enter, but barely large enough to hold her husband's girth. And within the open space was an amphora made of gold covered carvings depicting the constellations. A small golden plug sealed the mouth of the jar, and Allegra's heart jumped as she drew closer, certain now that he'd found what he'd been looking for.

Goran beckoned her over, his eyes sparkling with excitement and triumph. Above him the sun beat down on them, a glorious golden light bathing his face. And Allegra went, reluctant to leave him alone with his newfound treasure, desperate for the feel of his love, as though something deep inside her told her that the amphora had already taken possession of the man she loved more than life itself. "We found it, my love," he called out, smiling ever brighter as Allegra reached him. "It's real, and we have it," he said, the whispered words more of a hiss of excitement.

She'd never been fooled by his claims that the city itself was his goal.

Goran took her into his arms and Allegra curled her hands around his waist, pouring all her love into her embrace in the hopes that her husband would value their love as more important than his dreams of treasure hunting.

Alas, it was not meant to be.

The return trip to the ship was fraught with frustration as tempers flared among the sailors, as well as between Goran and Allegra. She had wondered on more than one occasion what could have been responsible for the destruction of the city, and as she watched her husband clutch tightly to the amphora, she grew more certain every moment that passed that the brass vessel may have something to do with the fall of Atlantis.

They boarded the ship, and the sailors all went their separate ways after one of the crew seemed to lose his mind. He'd begun to talk to himself even before they'd reached the ship, and his condition only grew worse after boarding. His ranting had upset the rest of the crew.

Arms still wrapped around the amphora, Goran escaped to their cabin, hiding there for most of the journey home. Allegra had spent half her journey pretending to be sleeping, the other half feigning nausea in order to be alone outside.

Goran never left the cabin the entire journey back to Delphi.

If that had not been a sure sign, Allegra didn't know what was.

CHAPTER 23

*W*aiting to find out more about when the trio of disasters was about to happen had begun to get on Allegra's nerves. In addition, the strange dream had also set her off balance, and she'd found herself rummaging around inside the fire-safe again, on the hunt for more information about the Pythia Lydia and her ill-fated romance with Goran, the hunter of lost cities.

The dream had ended a little too soon, and Allegra hoped that perhaps she would find a little more information on Lydia before the time came for the team to leave for the mission.

Max had relented eventually, agreeing that Allegra could go with Athena and Xales. Allegra was only too happy with having a powerful demigod and her own personal familiar on her team. She had little doubt that she'd be safer than Max and his team—which did seem a little unfair when she thought about it.

Marcus Asante, Max's second in command at FAPA had arrived with Flavius Lex. Marcus would help coordinate the searches and would head-up the Fornia investigation with his team back home, while Max would head to Pompeii with the seer. The man had seemed somewhat subdued, his startlingly blue eyes somewhat faded, and Allegra had to wonder if he too held her responsible for Corina's death. The way Allegra did.

Corina's death on their mission to Rajasthan to identify the origin point of the deadly flu had remained with Allegra, the seer's blood still staining her hands.

Allegra had come to terms with her condition, after some intensive research and coming to understand what she suffered from—a hysteria of sorts, something modern doctors defined as a long-term emotional reaction to any form of high-stress situation. Anyone from soldiers after battles to mothers who lose their babies, to rape victims and even victims of accidents and emotional abuse in a family setting, will suffer from such a hysteria.

And Allegra had recognized it in the visions of blood on her hands. She knew the blood was not real, even when she was compelled to soap and scrub her fingers sometimes until they bled. How she was going to resolve her feelings, she was not yet sure. It was possible that she'd need to speak to a therapist, but the last thing she needed was to cast any form of doubt upon the strength and power of the Pythia.

So she'd resolved to work out her feelings on her own.

And now, every time she saw the blood on her hands, she counted to ten and focused on Corina, first her personality, then her strong-mindedness. Allegra tried to reset her train of thought into one that accepted Corina's own actions, and that the seer had not been a victim but rather a woman within the agency, a woman with the power to make her own decisions, even if her choices had inevitably resulted in her death.

Allegra had to write the words down on a piece of paper, keeping it with her as much as was possible. Words that reminded her that Corina's death was not Allegra's fault, that the circumstances of the mission hadn't been within anyone's control. That there had been nothing she could have done to save Corina.

But it still struck her deeply that she'd not understood her vision of Corina's death, that the seer's passing had had nothing to do with the plague, that Allegra had not ultimately prevented it. But there was a truth Allegra had never admitted—although she was not technically supposed to be able to see another seer's future, she had done just that on the plane when they were traveling to Indus.

She had seen a snippet of Corina's future, one that at the time had not made much sense to Allegra. One that had only revealed its true nature when that fatal bullet had struck Corina, when the blood had spread across her shirt.

Which was why Allegra remained fixated on the fact that though she was after all the most powerful seer in the world, she had been incapable of saving the life of one of her own.

Allegra let out a weary sigh. Perhaps this was the next problem on her list that needed resolving. But for now, she had to focus herself on the task at hand—a triplicate of disasters and a strange vision of a troubled Pythia and her misguided Immunis that gave Allegra the strangest feeling of foreboding.

Taking a deep breath, Allegra closed the door of the fire-safe behind her and began to search the shelf one tome at a time. The names of the Pythias were written on the leather covers, some burned into the skin, some carved and inlaid with gold or silver, some stitched in golden thread.

After an hour—a time taken only because Allegra was terrified of rushing through the books and damaging them—she found the diary of the Pythia Lydia.

Allegra took the journal to the desk and opened it carefully, seating herself, pulling her chair close as she studied the first page.

I, Pythia Lydia, hereby record my time as the Oracle of Delphi, and do swear that the contents of this Codex be the starkest of truths, and the most honest of thoughts.

ALLEGRA PURSED HER LIPS. Perhaps she ought to have already begun her own codex. She too had a lot to write that would educate the next Pythia.

If there was a next Pythia.

Shaking the thought off, Allegra paged through Lydia's first musings, which turned out to be a record of her initiation into the Delphine Sanctum, and her first prophecies.

Lydia went on to describe her first meeting with Goran, a tradesman from the East who she'd met at a royal event, where diplomats, and the wealthy ate and danced with royalty. The oracle had recorded quite honestly her fascination with the enigmatic, worldly man, her attraction to his dark looks and his charming ways. Her initial observations were nothing like what Allegra had seen in the visions of the pair as they'd traveled to Atlantis.

GORAN EVET WAS NOT a man who swayed easily from his path. But the love of a woman was something far more powerful than ambition.

When Goran and I met for the first time, it had been easy to see that he'd been smitten instantly. To those who would claim that falling in love in the breath of a moment was impossible, I would have said they were nothing but fools, for Goran had only to set eyes upon me, to gaze upon my "olive skin and watch the light play upon my blushing cheeks, against my full red lips" and he was mine forever.

That I'd felt the same for him had been more than he could have ever asked for. In fact, Goran had truly believed our relationship would fall apart, that something terrible would happen to take me from his arms. But every day had passed with only more time to love me: the woman of his dreams.

Marriage had followed soon after, a joyous event in which the tribal council declared our marriage a holy union, had announced that the Seer's powers had become officially recognized both within Greece as well as around the world, and that Goran was to be declared Immunis.

Neither Goran nor I had known what that meant until the council had explained. One of the things about Goran that I had adored was that when I touched him, I saw nothing of his future. The council advised that such a mate to a Seer is Immune to the foretelling, making him the Immunis—a rather important, if not powerful—person who would stand at the Seer's side for the extent of her lifetime.

Later that year, the seat of the Seer was declared to be Delphi, and I, Lydia became known as the Pythia of Delphi. Goran and I had been happy in post-honeymoon bliss, until I received a strange vision. One that implied that the legendary city of Atlantis could be found out in the middle of the black seas of the Nerthallasus.

Filled with the passion of a curious explorer, Goran convinced me to help him find the city at least, assuring me that he had little interest in plundering, more in the fulfillment of a lifelong dream to see the fabled city of Atlantis with his own eyes.

Not long after this, we went on a long and somewhat arduous journey across the oceans in search of a city that had not been visited for thousands of years.

Yet, every step of the way, the vision proved to be correct, so accurate in fact that I would often upset the captain with my insistent instructions. Directions he'd at first declined to take, and had learned to his detriment, that the Seer's reputation preceded her for only one reason— she was never wrong. So he eventually set aside his measuring equipment and ceased his studying of the skies, giving himself and his entire crew over to the Pythia.

AND THEN, as Allegra turned the next delicate page, she came to Lydia's written account of that journey, descriptions that brought back the memory of Allegra's own vision so clearly.

Reading the words was akin to reliving the ancient Pythia's pain.

ALLEGRA SKIMMED the cramped text of Lydia's Codex until she reached the ancient Pythia's account of what had happened in the months after the couple had returned home to Delphi.

GORAN HAS BECOME OBSESSED with the amphora, spending long hours attempting to decipher the unknown script carved into the solid copper. He is convinced that the markings had some special meaning--of what he did not say. He wishes to keep it, but with my blessing. A part of me wishes he had proceeded without discussing it with me. What did he expect me to say other than the truth of how I feel, that stealing treasure is unlawful, a rule he ought not to break considering his status as Immunis? But I am now complicit, and should he proceed to drink from the amphora, he will do so under that guise of having received my blessing.

Goran is no longer the man that I once knew. He has grown angry, bitter, and almost as though he blames me for his own doubts as to whether opening the amphora is a good idea.

ALLEGRA READ FURTHER, her heart growing heavier with each paragraph of tightly spaced scrawl.

GORAN'S BEHAVIOR HAS CHANGED. He is no longer angry, nor does he mope around the villa either.

He is enthusiastic now, focused on his duties, returning to his old devotion to his Pythia. I am grateful for his return, but I take each day with a heavy dose of uncertainty as I know not what his obsession with the amphora will do to him. I feel the burden of his secret heavily, as I am unable to confide in anyone, as I know I will receive foremost their disapproval and only lastly their sympathy.

ALLEGRA SAT up and stared ahead at the wall. Lydia had been truly alone, and even her mentions of her life did not include Xales. Which meant that this particular Pythia had lived before Xales had been assigned to his protective duties.

With a deep sigh, Allegra returned to her reading, curious as to what was going to happen next, and inexplicably fearful.

THE VISIONS HAVE GROWN WORSE over these past months, the violence in them so vivid it is as though I myself am walking among the soldiers as they strike their swords and their spears deep within the flesh of their own brethren. I feel their agony, their pain, and their despair as though somehow, I am within their minds and their hearts too. Such visions are unknown to the priests, and they have expressed their concern, but the visions still come, many unbidden now, no longer requiring the ritual. Goran has retreated from me, a great distance divides us, a distance that remains one that I am not willing to cross.

The news results in many changes. The priests have placed the reason for my disturbing visions at the feet of the babe I am carrying. Goran has returned to me, the revelation that he is soon to be a father, has changed him. He is no longer distant, and has become more involved in the life of the pythia, taking his Immunis duties more seriously now. He prepares for the coming of the child as one would prepare for the birth of a king.

The priests are joyous too, the prospect of a new pythia bringing relief to them all as there were fears for the last decade that I would not bear a child. Perhaps that was what had caused Goran to withdraw. But I cannot attempt to unravel the puzzle that is my husband. He has admitted that he will not part with the amphora just yet, has promised to complete his studies and return the relic to the State. He swears he does not want anything to go wrong where his child is concerned.

ALLEGRA RUBBED HER FOREHEAD, aware that she was tracking dust across her face. The room had grown cold, and she rose to light the coals in the brazier beside the door. The coals caught alight quickly and soon the flames blazed. Allegra returned to the codex and turned the page.

THE BABE HAS ARRIVED, and no father and son have ever been so close. Goran has taken little Claudinius under his care, focusing his attention so much upon my son that the priests have accused him of neglecting his duties to the Pythia.

As much as I have defended Goran, I too feel the pain of loneliness. Perhaps as the boy grows, his father may return to me.

ALLEGRA TURNED A FEW MORE PAGES, tiring of the sadness of the story to a point that she felt a low ebb of depression beginning to pull at her. Shaking it off she focused on a new entry, one a few years later, after Lydia had born three more sons, Severianus, Aquilinus, and Iulius.

THE BOYS HAVE GROWN into young men, but there is something strange about them. They follow their sire around like a group of ducklings, ever waiting to receive a word of kindness or praise. I am glad to see their relationship is strong, that their bond is growing each day. My only sorrow is that Goran has again drifted from me. And as before, we have disagreed on his possession of the amphora. I dare not ask if he will at least hand it over to the documentor of the historical archives in Athens; he's turned to violence a number of times now, and I do not wish a repeat.

My last babe was lost to me, and I believe the child was killed within the womb during his last beating. Perhaps I should not have stood my ground. Had I been gentler, perhaps relented, and agreed with him, perhaps then my infant girl would have lived. The priests are disappointed in me, but they know nothing of my turmoil, nothing of the man my Goran has become.

He has turned my sons against me with his latent anger and his subtle insults. I often wonder what I have done to deserve this change in treatment at the hands of a man I once loved with all my heart. I am still fertile, my courses still come, and thus I am still of the age to bear another child. But the thought of lying with a man who has turned from a god to a monster, brings both shame and disgust. But how do I say no, how do I void the marriage bed when the husband may claim his right on his wife's body whenever he so wishes, Pythia or not.

ALLEGRA STIFFENED AND SAT BACK. Lydia's life had gone from brimming with love and happiness to something so filled with horror that Allegra felt as though she were reading a piece of fiction deliberately intended to tug at one's heartstrings.

She rubbed her forehead again and got to her feet, unable to read any further. Lydia's story would have to wait until Allegra was feeling a little more up to facing the horrors that the poor Pythia had suffered.

Allegra considered beginning her own codex right then and there, but the pull of fatigue and hunger was enough to change her mind. She left the room, the codex lying on the desk to await her return.

As she slipped back into the study, the darkness that greeted her was not surprising. She shut the door and checked the patio doors, making certain they were locked. Not that she needed to worry about security here on the estate. The place was unusually safe, which still didn't mean Allegra lapsed in her awareness.

She'd been caught unawares all too many times since she'd stepped into her role as the Pythia.

CHAPTER 24

*A*llegra wandered through the house, making her way to the kitchen in the hopes of finding something to eat before she passed out. She walked into the shadowed kitchen where a single candle flickered on the large wooden table that took center stage. The enormous clay one took the entire left wall, while an equally large fireplace warmed the kitchen, throwing golden light onto Mara who sat there, picking at a pile of shredded chicken and olives.

The backlighting cast odd shadows upon the old woman, transforming her into something bordering on demonic. Allegra startled and paused on the threshold, hand to her chest as her heartbeat spiked.

"Mara," Allegra said, exhaling slowing as she drew closer to the silent woman. "I didn't expect anyone to be here at this time of the night."

Mara smirked. "I knew you'd come looking for food eventually." She cocked her head at the clay oven. "Inside. Your plate is waiting for you."

"What's on the menu today?" asked Allegra even as she tugged open the door to the clay oven, releasing a flood of warmth that enveloped her, reminding her how cold she really was.

"Chicken pie with mushrooms and thyme. I think Gerda added potato to the mix as well." Mara shrugged, feigning indifference when Allegra knew all too well how hands-on the old woman was.

"Delicious," Allegra said as she inhaled the aroma of warm pastry and hot chicken. The cook had left a small pie for Allegra, sitting on a plate accompanied by a head of buttery mash. She set it on the table beside Mara and drew up a chair, unable to hold back the shiver that rippled through her as she tucked into the pie.

"You should not miss meals. It's not healthy."

"Sorry, Mara. I'll try to remember. I'm not sure how I lost track of time."

"Aurelia used to do the very same thing. Hide away in her study and then disappear for hours. Never told me where she went either," Mara muttered, her tone bearing a hint of resentment.

Allegra swallowed her bite of pie and tilted her head to look at Mara. "I'm sorry Mara. For me and Aurelia. Sadly, there are some things the Pythia must do alone. Being unable to share is about the hardest thing about this job for me. I imagine Aurelia felt the same way."

Mara let out a snort that was an odd amalgamation of scorn, regret, and affection. "She was so much like you when she first took on her role."

Allegra glanced at the old woman, curious now. "I don't know anything about her early days. Were you with her from the beginning?"

Mara nodded. "I was handmaiden to Pythia Cordelia who was Aurelia's predecessor. Aurelia was happy to keep me on, as I was well experienced with regard to the way the Pythia functions in relation to the demands of the countries of the world."

"Were you a liaison like Max?" asked Allegra, suddenly aware that she had no idea of Mara's origins. "Mara, where are you from? You've never told us anything about yourself."

The old woman shrugged. "You never asked," she said then waved a hand when Allegra's face fell as she realized the truth of those words. How callous of her to not attempt to get to know Mara. "Don't worry child. I'm not the easiest of people to communicate with. And besides, you've had much to deal with these past months."

Allegra smiled and continued to eat, making a rolling motion with her hand so Mara would keep talking.

Mara took a deep breath and got to her feet, walking slowly to a large door set into the stone wall. Inside was an array of wines both from the estate's vineyards and from around the world, a combination of gifts from various countries and of Aurelia's own selections.

She retrieved a bottle of cabernet merlot and popped the cork. Setting it before Allegra, she fetched two wine goblets from the shelves behind her and proceeded to pour them each a glass. Allegra waited patiently, enjoying the silence and the meal, not wanting to push the old woman any harder than she was ready to.

Mara sat down, took a sip and swished the wine around her mouth, gargling the wine before swallowing it. Allegra choked back her laughter and focused on eating and swallowing, avoiding the old woman's eyes.

Then, Mara cleared her throat and said, "I became hand-maiden to Cordelia when I was fourteen. The Pythia Cordelia was born in a small Welsh town in the Brittanic Isles, and the priests of the Pythian order insisted on allocating a handmaiden to Cordelia from the outset of her reign."

Reign? Odd word to use to describe the oracle's role, thought Allegra as she sipped the deliciously sweet wine.

"As niece to Cordelia, the role came to me without much

question. The handmaiden's duties were no longer that of the ancient ones who served the Pythia. In those times, the handmaiden would perform every task for her Pythia, from bathing to dressing, to performing all personal servant functions like emptying out bedpans, mending clothes. But over the years the role of handmaiden began to transform into one more of a communications or secretarial role. I was very pleased to be selected, even though it was likely I would never find a husband because of it."

"Oh? Is there a rule precluding marriage for a handmaiden?"

Mara shook her head. "No rule as such, but men take second place to everything. It would have been difficult to find a man who was strong enough in personality to accept having a wife who spent the majority of her time with another woman. Even having a family would have meant merely birthing the babe and passing it on to someone else to raise. A difficult choice but one that many handmaidens have made through the centuries.

"Cordelia was most unhappy as she did not want to stop me from having a family, but I made it clear that I would only consider a husband who would accept us both," Mara said, letting out a loud laugh. "Cordelia thought that was quite funny, but over the years we came to understand the truth of it."

"Did she have a family?"

"Yes. Cordelia bore two infants, Richard and Helena, both grew to adulthood. Helena did not possess the power of the oracle. I believe Cordelia was relieved at the time, but she lived a long and tiring life, and I know she often wished that things had been different."

"How so?"

"It's much better for the oracle herself if she passed her reign on to the next oracle and still had some life left to live. Being a Pythia does tend to control one's life, as I'm sure you know. Just as you have struggled against the bonds, so do most Pythias."

"So how did you serve Cordelia?"

Mara smiled and glanced down at her wine goblet. "I studied a lot. I learned about the social and political climate of the time, helped Cordelia make decisions on how best to voice the visions she received."

Allegra schooled her features, incredibly impressed as she stared at Mara. The ancient woman had once been within the hub of world political agendas, a fact that Allegra would never have guessed.

Another reason why it paid never to judge another person solely on your own impressions.

CHAPTER 25

*A*llegra frowned. "I know that some of the governments who have rights to the oracles' visions are likely to use them for nefarious means, but why not just say you saw nothing?"

The old woman chuckled, then slugged back the rest of her wine. "Cordelia did take that route, more times than I can recall. But many of her visions were helpful to the people, more than to the governments, so it became an intricate dance in how to present the visions in order to ensure those governmental representatives would act out of the interest of their people while still believing they acted in their own interests."

"See, that is why I always said I never wanted to be in politics."

"Sadly, my child, the role of the Pythia is largely political."

"Aurelia didn't make it seem that way. How did she come to the role?"

"Cordelia was taken by the terrible pox of 3053, a disease she'd warned the world of. Too few paid attention and the result was the death of thousands of people, including Cordelia and her family."

"All of them," Allegra asked, horrified.

Mara nodded. "It was a terrible time."

"I remember learning about that. It was around sixty years ago."

Mara cleared her throat then reached for the wine bottle, her movements a sequence of jerks. "When Cordelia died, they searched for a Pythia and thankfully it didn't take long before Aurelia's powers manifested. She was quite resistant to the idea of having her life taken away from her, her independence, her husband. Aurelia didn't take kindly to being the Pythia, but the pox made the decision for her. After her husband died, she succeeded Cordelia with little complaint."

"She would have been what...around twenty-three?" Allegra said, tapping the side of her wine goblet.

Mara nodded. "Despite the burden of grief she bore when she took on the role, Aurelia became one of the most powerful and respected Pythias in the modern age. But she soon tired of the job, and began to search for a replacement. Until she found you. I'm still not sure how she tracked you down. I recall Aurelia saying over and over that the Pythian line was dead, that it had been decimated leaving no Oracle alive. And yet, one day she comes to me and announces that she'd found the next Pythia and that she was going to keep her safely hidden until Aurelia's own time came to an end. I think she held on only because she was waiting for you to be ready."

Allegra squinted at Mara. "And how in the world would she have known that?"

Mara stared at Allegra for a long moment. "Aurelia became Pythia at the age of twenty-three," she said, a repetition Allegra ignored. "She had only been Pythia for two months when she discovered she was with child."

"And the father died in the plague," said Allegra, a blanket of sadness surrounding her.

Mara shook her head. "Aurelia delivered a beautiful, healthy boy in the spring of the following year. But under the circumstances, she could not keep the child, and she gave him up for adoption."

Allegra poured herself another glass of wine, turning over Mara's implication. "Are you trying to say that Aurelia's son is somehow connected to me? Did Aurelia have him keeping an eye on me?"

The old woman smirked. "You could say that."

Allegra stiffened mid-swallow, her eyes widening as it hit her what Mara was implying. The wine went down the wrong way, and she choked then coughed hard, the alcohol going up her nose, making her eyes burn.

"Dad?" Allegra managed to set her glass on the table before falling into a second fit of coughing while Mara merely looked on, smiling. At last, Allegra ceased coughing and patted her chest while clearing her throat. "Aurelia is my grandmother?" she asked.

But even as the words left her mouth, and even as Mara gave a tiny shake of her head, Allegra understood. Aurelia had entrusted Jocasta's child to someone close enough to her that she could trust, but someone who had no known connection to a Pythia.

"I'm assuming my adoption was a setup?" asked Allegra, marveling at Aurelia's smarts. Allegra reached for her glass and took a sip, hoping the wine would quell some of her nerves.

"Aurelia did put you up for adoption, and legally it was a secret arrangement, but things were structured in such a way that Aurelia would be allowed to choose the family. Aleks and Diana were approached by an intermediate, undisclosed party, and it was suggested they make the application."

"Undisclosed party as in you?" Allegra pointed a finger at Mara, taking care not to tip her wine glass over.

Mara merely smirked.

"I'm assuming Aurelia never lost touch with Dad?"

"No. She was not the kind of mother who could possibly relinquish her connection with her child. But she spent a lifetime mourning his loss. She missed his formative years, his milestones, everything that she wanted to share with him."

Allegra blinked, understanding now what Aurelia had meant when she'd said she understood what it meant to be parted from a child. Tears burned Allegra's eyes as she felt a surge of sorrow for the old Pythia who had ultimately saved Allegra's life.

"She did so much for me, and I never got to thank her."

"She didn't need thanks. She knew she was doing the right thing."

Allegra swallowed hard. "Did she come to the funeral? I don't remember seeing her."

"We were both there, child. But you wouldn't have noticed. You were distraught, and it broke Aurelia's heart to see you in so much pain."

Allegra sniffed back the fresh wave of tears that now threatened to spill as she thought of her beloved father. "She would have been nursing her own broken heart. Why would she have felt bad for me?"

Mara didn't reply, and a silence followed that was filled with a sense of despair.

Then Allegra downed the last of her wine and set the glass on the table. "I'd rather not think about him. Or Mother. Every day that goes by is another day that it hurts. And now...now I have to remember that they were not my real parents." Allegra sighed and then smiled, accepting that deep down her biological connection to Aleks and Diana Damascus was irrelevant because her love for them was pure and true.

Mara's voice cut into Allegra's musings. "You know you can select a handmaiden now if you want."

Brow furrowed, Allegra leaned toward Mara. "What do you mean? Are you no longer up to being my handmaiden?"

The old woman cackled heartily. "The truth is I want to be selfish and say I'm well and truly capable of performing my duties as handmaiden, but the reality is I've grown far too old.

This body is tired, and there are times when my mind fades. Besides, I haven't performed the role of handmaiden in over a decade. Once Aurelia moved here to the estate, she stopped her political shenanigans and only took visitors a few times a year. She'd grown weary of the world, of the greed and ambition, and she began to separate herself from that world in which she felt she no longer belonged. She used to say that she was a throwback to a past long dead with no hope of resurrection."

Allegra smiled and shook her head. She was about to say that she wished she could have spoken to Aurelia when it hit her whose voice she'd heard while she'd been submerged in the lake.

She was barely aware of Mara leaving the table and taking the dirty dishes with her, only startling when the old woman called to her from the threshold. "Perhaps you may want to look at Athena as a replacement for me. I think she will do a good job. I would have suggested Celestra but...I think perhaps her connection to Max will not always be nothing to bother you. Besides, it's about time he got his act together."

"What do you mean?" asked Allegra, clamping her hand over her mouth as she yawned widely.

Mara snickered. "The man has more responsibilities than merely walking around with the title of Immunis, you know," she said before ambling down the hallway leaving a stunned Allegra staring into the darkness.

The secret that Max had wanted to tell Allegra all this time. The same secret that she'd told him she'd wait to hear when he was ready to tell it.

Max was Immunis.

And the Immunis was the mate to the Pythia.

CHAPTER 26

*M*ax stared at Allegra as she stood motionless inside his tiny office, her cheeks red, her eyes wide. He'd expected her to be angry. Instead, she looked like she was about to burst into tears.

"Why did you not tell me?" she asked softly, her gaze meeting Max's for the briefest moment before flitting away and studying the painting of a bland hillside that Mara had dropped off—the old woman's unspoken suggestion that he may want to spruce the office up a bit.

Max smiled sadly and waved a hand at Allegra's face. "This is the reason I didn't say anything. Because the knowledge would come with a sense of obligation, and then perhaps with a sense of rebellion," Max let out a weary sigh and sank into his chair. "Trust me, I know how that feels. I engaged in a bit of rebellion myself on discovering what Immunis truly meant."

Max smiled at the memory, although even now there was nothing about that day that was amusing. Aurelia had seemed to enjoy imparting the knowledge, and she'd merely watched, her expression inscrutable as Max had refused point blank to agree.

Now her shoulders shortened and she shifted on her feet, then settled into the single chair in front of Max's desk, her expression neutral.

Max decided to keep talking. "After Aurelia told me what I was meant to do—as in be the husband of the Pythia—I got angry. I got furious. I left and told her to go to Hades, and that I was not going to live my life as a pawn in someone else's game. I asked Les to move in with me after that, and I often think about what that had meant about me and my own selfish needs."

"You were angry and hurt. Of course, you would have reacted."

"But it was more than that. The knowledge was too much, and instead of trying to deal with my rejection of that burden, I proceeded to hurt the people around me. Human nature is cruel more than we like to admit." Max glanced out of his patio doors, staring off into the distant past, regret lining his face as he let out a soft sigh. "I used her to act out my frustration and anger against what I perceived as an unwilling burden placed on my shoulders. I gave Les the impression that there was a future for us, but I was lying to her, and more importantly, I was lying to myself."

Allegra pursed her lips, her eyes now sad. "You could have just told Aurelia that you'll stay with her but that you won't marry anyone under duress," she countered, her eyes still expressionless. For the first time, Max was unable to identify what she was feeling—which was a really bad sign. "I'm sure she would have listened."

Max snorted. "Did you not realize as yet that you are the very last of the Pythias? It's supposed to be some sort of familial obligation for you to procreate. I didn't think you'd be in any way ready to jump into bed with your allocated Immunis just for the purposes of conception."

Allegra made a rude sound. "So are we supposed to make babies regardless of how we feel about it?"

"That about sums it up," said Max, somewhat amused at the expression on Allegra's face.

She shook her head. "That sounds quite mercenary and distasteful. Although for some reason I can imagine that act of intercourse was something the old priests would have wanted proof of." A mischievous smile turned her lips up at the corners.

Max chuckled. "Fortunately, there will be no witnesses because there will be no on-demand procreation."

Allegra folded her arms and met Max's gaze. "What if that procreation has already taken place?"

Eye's widening, Max leaned forward. "Are you—"

"No. I'm not pregnant. I just meant…oh, I don't know what I meant. This is all too much to process." Allegra got to her feet and paced a short path before Max's desk. "I suppose this would have been way easier to say no to if we weren't already…involved."

A grin spread on Max's face. "So we're *involved* then?" He quirked an eyebrow.

Allegra pointed a finger at Max. "You be quiet. I'm trying to think."

"Well, I do believe we have better things to think about than forced procreation."

"Which is?" Asked Allegra.

"Confirmation of tectonic activity in all three of our locations."

"Guess that's our cue then," Allegra said as she turned to head for the door. On the threshold, she paused and looked over her shoulder. "You do know there is another method of conception, should the on-demand intercourse not be to your liking?" she said, failing to hold back a smile.

"Oh?" Max asked, his eyes dancing with amusement.

Allegra nodded. "I believe a fair number of humans have been conceived in-vitro. That's an option…should the need ever arise," she said then sauntered off into the passage.

Allegra had to hold back a burst of laughter as Max's words drifted out into the hall, accompanied by a disgusted growl. "I'll be damned if any child of mine is ever conceived in a petri dish. Not while the equipment is still working."

CHAPTER 27

*A*s planned, the three teams headed out in their respective directions with Allegra feeling a pang of homesickness at the thought that she'd been so close to going back home, even if it had meant the reason was the destruction of everything she knew and loved.

In the end, she'd admitted to herself that the last thing she wanted to witness first hand was the annihilation of her place of birth. If that translated to cowardice, then Allegra would be happy to accept the title.

Allegra and Athena had taken the Pythia's plane, while Max arranged a chopper to take him and Flavius—who had remained behind after Marcus had returned to the States—to the island of Hawaii where they would grab a plane out to Pompeii.

Max had opted to avoid the Nova Roma airport; despite it being the quickest transit, he had insisted the three teams had to move under the radar of Aulus and the president of the NGS. Especially while on NGS soil.

The evening before, the three groups had spent a subdued few hours where numerous moments of conversation had punctuated stretches of long, uncomfortable silences.

Even Mara had been unusually quiet as she'd coordinated the delivery of the dinner courses, having prepared a special meal for their last night.

Allegra considered Mara's silence and had to assume the old woman had been thinking about their midnight conversation in the kitchen. Allegra hoped so, because she had to wonder if Mara had performed her dramatic revelation deliberately, revealing Max's truth before he'd been ready to.

Why she would have felt the need to do so was something Allegra accepted she may not ever know. Mara was a complicated woman, that much Allegra already knew. Perhaps Aurelia's handmaiden had felt that Max had been taking far too long.

Which he had.

And then there was the additional issue of addressing Mara's suggestion of choosing a new handmaiden in the old woman's stead. Mara was right; it was time to select someone to take her place, more so while she still remained capable of imparting her enormous stores of knowledge and experience.

Was Athena the right person for the role? Or was Les the better choice, even if her previous relationship with Max could pose a future complication? Allegra felt no envy or jealousy toward Max's ex, and didn't see herself evolving into a petty old woman, but Mara did have a point; there was sufficient potential for things to get problematic, which required Allegra take it seriously.

In the end, Allegra had come to agree that it was advisable to avoid the potential problem entirely. Sometimes, best intentions were the worst starting points for important decisions.

The flight had been long, during which time Allegra had read portions of Aurelia's codex. She'd been afraid to take the ancient books with her on the plane but had decided that if the plane went down, she herself would be dead, so it wouldn't matter all that much especially considering that Allegra was the last of the Pythias.

Aurelia's writings were detailed, and quite beautiful, her descriptions and voice bringing her experiences to life before Allegra's eyes.

I WRITE this with a heavy heart.

We arrived at Mt Fuji after a long and often perilous journey. Amidst the first falls of the winter snow, Mara and I arrived in Jipangu, intent on helping to save the people who live around the Suwanosejima volcano. Although we succeeded in evacuating the towns closest to the volcano, and although the seismologists monitored the fluctuating seismic activity around and within the volcano, all agreeing as to the likelihood that an eruption was imminent, we were all so very wrong.

And perhaps I would have happily accepted being wrong—even when I am never wrong, such is the accuracy of my visions. Had it not been for Kueishan Dao's destruction. I was so very very wrong. I cannot understand what went wrong, what I'd interpreted so incorrectly that I'd predicted an eruption in the wrong country.

I will bear the responsibility for all those lives lost on the island until my dying day.

I am afraid this failure has made me terribly afraid. I cannot trust my visions. How can I continue to be the Pythia if my visions prove so destructively false?

ALLEGRA'S EYES widened at the sadness that had flowed off the page. Aurelia had suffered because of this failure. And Allegra was glad for having read it at all. To know that the Oracle of Delphi could also get a prediction wrong, was something that provided Allegra with a great amount of relief.

ON THEIR ARRIVAL on the island of Bali, Athena had alighted from the plane first to perform a security sweep while Xales remained at Allegra's side inside the cabin until they'd received the all-clear. The Balinese authorities had been most accommodating, and Allegra had marveled at the treatment in comparison to her arrival in Qusqu not too long ago. Save for meeting Athena, Allegra would have readily skipped that episode in her experiences as the Pythia.

Both Athena and Xales had attempted to help Allegra with her luggage. She'd shrugged them off, muttering something about not being incapable, before stalking off toward the waiting hotel transport Jeep. The pair had followed in solemn silence and Allegra had begun to wonder if Xales in human form was a good development or not.

The air-conditioned interior of their vehicle was a welcome change to the heat of the day, heat that lingered despite the early evening in which they'd arrived.

Max had booked a suite at the same hotel where Pedro was staying—the Raja of Buleleng Resort and Spa—and was now beginning to wonder if perhaps there really was no danger to the community after all. Could Allegra have been as wrong as Aurelia had with Suwanosejima? But, Allegra had only her visions to go on, and so far she'd trusted in them, and she hadn't been wrong. Yet.

Still, she didn't have any other means to verify the truth of her visions and the teams had to perform their tasks as though the Pythia's word was really the ultimate truth.

After checking in, Athena had done a small bit of evening recon and discovered that the string of luxurious seaside hotels were all fully booked, meaning that if the wave did really come, they were looking at thousands of deaths in a matter of seconds.

Since their arrival in Bali, Allegra had been on edge, constantly fidgeting, her nerves making her feel as though something was very wrong. After a night of little sleep she'd awakened at dawn, and showered and changed, had even submitted to the hotel's complimentary massage therapist. But in the end, she'd felt the same.

Incomplete.

And filled with a strange sense of longing.

Oddly enough, the intensity of the feeling eased when Allegra had ventured out onto the sand from the patio doors of their suite. Their entire lodgings possessed room-to-sea access and stunning views of the water.

And as Allegra stood there, hands hanging at her sides, staring out at the water, digging her toes deep into the sand, she felt that pull again, a strange urge to move closer to the water.

An urge that, no matter how hard she resisted, Allegra seemed unable to suppress.

ALLEGRA WAS STANDING at the edge of the water, where the waves touched the sand. She stared around her, well aware of the reasons why these islands were the holiday destination of the world for centuries. She'd been meaning to visit the place, but her role as the Pythia had destroyed any holiday plans she may have entertained, past, present, or future. For all she knew, fighting the disasters of the future would negate the opportunity for relaxation for the duration of her tenure as the Pythia.

Now, she stood and stared out at the water, a tension building up deep inside her as she tried to understand when and how the tsunami would hit the resort. Allegra swallowed the ripple of unease as she took another step into the waves. The warm water was sublime, and soon Allegra found herself immersed waist deep within the sea. A glance over her shoulder confirmed that Athena had discovered Allegra's destination and was walking down the shallow path between the dunes, holding her hand to her eyes as she stared at Allegra who chuckled as she imagined the demigod's expression of displeasure. She hadn't meant to run off, well aware of the need for safety. So she stayed where she was, and waited for Athena to come to her.

A few moments later, Athena was splashing through the waves, scowling at Allegra. "You disappeared."

"I'm sorry. I didn't mean to. It's just..." Allegra turned to look out at the blue horizon, "...something about the water seems to be pulling me toward it." She'd spoken almost to her herself, but Athena's grunt of annoyance broke through her semi-trance, and Allegra looked over her shoulder at the demigod.

"More reason to let me know where in Hades' name you are going. We can't afford to assume your life is not in danger, Allegra." Athena shook her head, then turned to scan the shoreline. Beachgoers were scattered along the shoreline for a mile up and down the beach, children playing in the sand, swimmers cavorting in the waves and a few people walking along the sand. A perfectly tranquil afternoon, but that meant nothing in the scheme of things.

"I'm sorry. I'll try to be more aware," Allegra said, her gaze going back to the water.

From the side of her vision, she caught Athena turning to look at her. "What is it?" she asked, beginning to understand that there was something more going on than the need for rebellion.

Allegra shook her head. "I'm not entirely sure. Something urged me here...not sure why."

"Well, if anything, it includes swimming." Athena's comment was dry and filled with amusement.

Allegra glanced back at the demigod in time to see her deliberately scanning Allegra's black bathing suit. "You came dressed appropriately."

Allegra frowned and looked down at her swimwear. "I didn't even know...How odd." She looked back out to the water.

"What do you suppose this means?" asked Athena taking a step past Allegra as she shaded her eyes again.

"I feel like it means I need to venture deeper inside. I think...I think I may need to swim out toward whatever is calling me."

Athena let out a derisive snort. "And what do we do if this is just a call to you to swim to your death?"

Allegra hesitated. "Where is Xales?"

"Disappeared, so I'm assuming he's around and watching you."

Allegra looked around her. "Xales?"

The air shimmered in front of Allegra, and the haze from of the boar-man appeared. He'd materialized only partially, his glamor ensuring his appearance would go unnoticed by any observers around them. "I am here, my lady."

"What do you think?" she asked him softly.

The familiar looked out at the ocean again. "I do not feel like this option is dangerous for you, but I cannot see the future," he said with a smirk. Then he shook his head. "In any case, I will go with you, so should you go underwater, I shall still remain at your side. You are quite safe with me."

"I don't deny that, but I'm coming too," said Athena, armed crossed over her own swimsuit. She too had dressed accordingly.

"What if I have to go under?"

"Then I'll come with you."

"Can you breathe underwater?"

She shrugged. "When the need arises. Demigod...I'll be fine."

Allegra lifted an eyebrow. "And what if you are not fine?"

"Then I shall pay the price." Athena shifted to face Allegra head-on. "I am going to say this now, before we go into the water —because I am coming with you. I am making this decision because it is my choice. I know Xales is going with you, and I know you have to go, because I feel like this must have something to do with the tsunami you saw. So in the interests of keeping you safe as well as making sure we find out everything we need to know about the disaster, I am coming with you. If I fail to return alive—unlikely, might I add—it will be my own choice. You are not responsible for my decisions."

There was a long silence in which Allegra simply stared at the demigod's implacable expression.

At last, she inhaled deeply. "Very well. Though I cannot promise that should this prove a journey that will cost you your life, I will not feel free of the responsibility."

"I understand. Just don't be too hard on yourself," Athena said with an airy wave.

Allegra chuckled as both the women turned to stare out at the azure sea.

"Well, this is it," Allegra said as she began to wade deeper into the water.

Athena followed, and the pair swam further and further into the ocean, until the waves began to lift them off the ocean floor.

"What now?" Athena asked scanning the waves around them.

Behind them the shore was a thin line on the horizon and water surrounded them, almost enough to terrify Allegra. She took another deep breath, and as she treaded water and paddled with her hands, her fingers brushed against Xales' fur. She sucked in a breath. "Now we need to dive."

"Are you certain? Perhaps we could just wait here until we figure out what is next?" suggested Athena, concern darkening her green eyes.

"No. It's time. We don't have all the time in the world in which to make this decision. That eruption or whatever it was can happen at any moment."

Athena nodded, defeated. "Very well. I'm ready when you are,"

Allegra reached out and touched the demigod's shoulder. "I meant to ask you to be my handmaiden, but I kept not getting a chance."

"And you think now is the best moment to make such a proposal," Athena asked grinning.

"I take it the idea is something you approve of?"

Athena nodded. "I admit I never considered it as a possibility. Or anything...I didn't even entertain the thought." the demigod grinned. "I'll be happy to be your handmaiden Pythia Allegra. Now let's get out of this alive, and I'll ask Mara to start my training."

Athena was muttering something about being worried about the training because Mara was so scary, and Allegra smiled as she sank into the water.

CHAPTER 28

*A*s Allegra sank deeper into the water, the throbbing need within her began to lessen, but only by a small fraction, giving her a sense that she was moving in the right direction. A part of her mind rebelled at the thought that she was ultimately being controlled by some unknown force, and thereby also endangering Athena's life. But she had no sense that the call was something she should be worried about. The feelings within her, though jumbled, felt safe.

Which in the end, meant nothing at all.

Allegra's lungs sparked with pain as she swam deeper into the water, leaving behind the azure blue and descending into inky blackness. Athena swam beside her, and a glance at the demigod confirmed that she wasn't struggling as badly as Allegra would have guessed. Perhaps she was right, and her demigod genes would help her get through to their destination.

Wherever that was.

Minutes passed, and Allegra began to struggle, her chest tight and throbbing now, as though her heart were about to burst right out of her chest. Xales was beside her the entire way and seemed to sense her desperation, shooting forward and pulling Allegra along. He was implying he'd take her where she wanted to go, but she wasn't about to leave Athena behind.

She glanced over her shoulder at the demigod who was swimming beside her, and beckoned her closer. Athena obeyed and angled toward Allegra, following her instructions to hold onto Xales. The moment she grasped the boar's fur, he looked pointedly at Allegra.

She stared off into the depths and pointed down to the left, to where the pull seemed strongest.

Without responding, Xales began to swim, faster than Allegra could have hoped for. Her hair streamed behind her, and she had to hold onto the wrap at her waist. A glance over Xales' shoulder revealed Athena was in the same situation and looked exhilarated to boot. Her eyes sparkled as she grinned at Allegra.

Grinning back, Allegra refocused on the magnetic pull, patting Xales to indicate that he could aim straight ahead. With her lungs bursting, Allegra soon began to see the flickering of starbursts in her vision, the edges going slowly darker and darker. Athena grabbed her hand, and Allegra looked over at her, head lolling. The demigod tugged hard at Allegra's hand, scowling at her, urging her to stay awake.

Shaking her head, Allegra focused harder on the depths of the ocean, but only seconds later she felt as though she was never going to make it. With nothing in sight, and her lungs exploding, her vision blurring, and her consciousness ebbing, she knew she may have made a huge mistake.

She tugged on Xales, and he came to a halt, both he and Athena throwing questioning glares at her. She shook her head and pointed up at the surface, stabbing at the top frantically.

Athena's expression darkened, and she shook her head, but Xales seemed to agree, and he began to turn away. Allegra spun around and kicked upward and was about to pull on Xales and request a faster ascent when Athena disappeared. For a moment,

Allegra felt panic flood her veins, and she spun around, terrified that something had happened to the demigod. Instead, she spotted Athena a few feet away, her eyes widening as Allegra beckoned frantically, pointing at the depths again and shaking her head.

Startled, Allegra looked below her, and almost sucked in a lungful of air when she spotted a glow emanating from the murky depths. She tugged at Xales, who obeyed and began to pull her toward Athena. Allegra wasn't sure how long they'd been diving, but she knew it was far longer than her usual three minutes. She had to wonder what was giving her the extra ability to withstand such an extended period of time without oxygen.

But her mind was pulled away from those practical thoughts when she found herself slamming into what appeared to be a greenish-blue dome under the sea. And no slamming happened.

The trio passed right through the barrier and were still conscious and alive despite Allegra's fears.

A blurry figure flashed past Allegra, and she swirled to follow the creature's movements, only to find herself turning to face a strange man.

The edges of his body glowed as though his body was a living lightbulb. His green eyes were somber as he nodded slowly at Allegra then said, "You may breathe."

Allegra shook her head and glanced over at Athena who also shook her head.

The man chuckled, making Allegra wonder how it was possible that he could speak underwater. Then she blinked as he looked over at Athena. "My dear Athena, for a goddess who has such a depth of faith in me, it seems you have in fact failed to recognize me."

Athena's eyes widened, and she coughed, breathing in the water around her. A terror-filled moment went by—during which Allegra had to wonder where it was wise to just believe anything the stranger said—and then Athena let out a self-depre-cating laugh.

"I apologize, my lord," she said as she bowed low.

Allegra's gaze flashed toward the god, accepting now what the strange glow meant. She took a breath of the water and coughed, shaking her head in disbelief. "I apologize, my lord. I should have trusted you."

Neptune smiled, the expression benevolent. "My dear Pythia. I don't believe you have any reason to believe me. I have, after all, attempted to kill you once before."

The god's words seemed to swirl around Allegra, and for a moment she felt faint. Then she glanced over at Athena, shifting her eyes pointedly at the god, her actions saying, "See, I was right."

Athena frowned and focused on Neptune. "My Lord, did you truly make an attempt to kill the Pythia?"

Neptune tipped his head forward, his expression sad. "I will discuss this further once we are in safer territory. The seabed is far too unstable for us to remain here out in the open. I promise to explain, and I believe you will understand."

"I'm to trust a god who just admitted he'd tried to kill me?"

Neptune shrugged and began to swim away. "I'm not trying to kill you anymore, if that helps."

Then he was gone, and Allegra found herself carried along as Xales pulled her forward. Athena snagged a handful of the boar's pelt just in time, and the pair held on for dear life as Xales sped through the water following the path taken by Neptune.

Allegra was a little unsure of what had just happened.

One, the powerful magnetic force that had been calling to her, had come from the god of the sea.

And two, that same god had once tried to kill Allegra.

She was pretty sure that the smartest move should have been to make a beeline for the surface and get the hell out of Neptune's domain.

Then why was she willingly following Neptune deeper into his world?

Allegra shook her head. Perhaps this was one decision she'd have to keep from Max.

Maybe Athena could take responsibility, she was the hand-maiden to the pythia after all.

CHAPTER 29

*D*espite Allegra's reservations, she found herself still alive and being guided into a dark rocky cavern, one that seemed to have appeared out of nowhere as they swam through water so deep that she was surrounded by blackness. Had it not been for the subtle glow emanating from the green dome above, she was sure she would not have been able to see anything.

Xales drew to a stop as Neptune turned and hovered in front of what looked like a golden gate. As they drew closer, Allegra was amazed to see that the gate was not gold. Instead, it appeared to be constructed from a pearlescent substance that gave off an iridescent glow. With the movement of the water, and the glow from above, the gate shimmered and appeared to sparkle with every color of the rainbow.

Neptune extended a hand in front of the gate, and the enormous gate opened slowly, allowing the trio to enter before he followed and shut it behind them.

Allegra hesitated for the briefest moment, aware now that there really was no turning back. They were deep underwater, locked beneath a magical dome, and now trapped behind an enormous gate. If Neptune had wanted to trap Allegra, he'd certainly managed it without much trouble.

But the God of the Sea appeared to be the nicest of villains, guiding them toward a small hall, the floor of which was made of the same pale iridescent substance as the gate. Here though they formed great irregular marble-like tiles forked with gold and silver. The floor was raised and was surrounded by nine pillars, making the structure look quite similar to a Greek temple, no surprise given this was Neptune's hall.

They swam up to it, and then settled onto the floor, as though they were no longer floating. So strange to ignore the fact that she was breathing underwater.

Neptune waved to a large oval table and seated himself opposite Allegra. She noted that the god did not select the head of the table for a seat, and Allegra responded by sitting in the seat facing Neptune. Leaving Athena and Xales hovering.

"Sit, please. We do not stand on ceremony here," he said waving a hand over the table.

As he moved his hand, a selection of platters appeared on the table filled with an array of unrecognizable delicacies. None of which appealed to Allegra—who needed to think about eating while inhaling and exhaling the ocean.

Allegra shook her head, ignoring Athena's pointed glare. Clearly declining the god's offer was rude, but Allegra didn't have the time to be wined and dined before finding out why Neptune had called her to him.

The god gave a nod. "I apologize for the subterfuge. I don't resort to using the power to compel a mortal to come to me very often. I find it most distasteful."

"As distasteful as trying to kill me?" Allegra asked, to a chorus of shocked gasps. She ignored them and lifted her chin. Too late to apologize and go back on her words now.

~

ALLEGRA LIFTED her chin and met the god's eyes. And found him smiling, his lips pursed as he shook his head.

"I must apologize, my lady Pythia. For the longest time, I've been led down the wrong path, believing, as so many do, that the Pythia is bad for humanity, that her very existence is leading to much of the terrible events in this world."

Allegra frowned. "Why would you have thought such a thing? Has a Pythia ever threatened you?"

Neptune rested against the back of his chair. "The world must exist in balance. The Pythia's visions have seemed to upset that balance."

"Because a natural disaster is an act of nature and by averting it, we may be thwarting the very basic nature of nature." Allegra smiled as she spoke, understanding Neptune's point only too well.

"I see you share my position. It had been the very basis for much of the decisions in the last few centuries. There was a time when I did believe that the Pythia stood for the benefit of the mortals, but that was back when the Sybils were speaking the words of Apollo."

"But were they not said to have been intoxicated at the time, merely speaking what their drug-induced illusions told them to?" asked Allegra.

Neptune nodded. "In all things, there is the truth, and the reality behind that truth."

"That's a lie?"

"In ancient times, mortals found it extremely hard to accept that one of their own could access the future, could tell even the most powerful of men that their lives would go a certain way unless they avoided the choices that would lead them down that path. But the flaw in that is that people also wanted to know what their future holds. So, a person who has the ability to predict the future is also a danger to a mortal. The power of the oracle was an almost god-like one, and mortals were uncomfortable with the thought that one of their own peers could be this powerful naturally. The gods believed the best way to soothe the discomfort of those mortals who could rebel against the oracle's power was to engender the impression that the words were those of the gods themselves."

"Which is when Apollo decided to be the oracle's guardian?" asked Athena, her brow furrowed as she thought it over. "So, the gods decided that the oracle would be drugged?"

Neptune laughed loudly. "The Pythia was never really drugged. Herbs were burned yes, but there were two sets of herbs, those that intoxicated the Pythia and those that left her clearheaded."

Allegra let out a low gasp. "The oracles didn't always have the power to tell the future," she said softly, lifting an eyebrow, both surprised and impressed. "That's a tale that had withstood centuries of retellings."

Neptune nodded. "Apollo was forced on a few occasions to appear to the oracle and tell her a few semi-critical pieces of information so she would appear to be a true seer."

"And of course, that would have perpetuated the myth that Apollo was the giver of the visions."

"And the gods were only too happy to help perpetuate it ever since. But a line of Oracles grew, seers with real power to see the future, not randomly selected women for which the priests had to search far and wide."

"And that line began the daughters of Pythia?"

Neptune nodded. "The first of them was Lydia, whose children were all born male and without power."

"Then how did the line of the pythia develop? I didn't know the pythia's received their powers through a paternal connection."

"They don't," said Neptune enigmatically.

Allegra stared at the god, her mind racing as she attempted to throw a few pieces together. And then, as she considered Lydia's terrible predicament, she came to only one conclusion.

Lydia had a daughter.

CHAPTER 30

*A*llegra let out a chuckle. "Lydia had a female child."

Neptune nodded. "She gave the infant away to Lucia, a seer who was also in the line of succession to become the next Pythia. Lucia, in turn, transferred Kassandra into the care of a Trojan family and the infant remained hidden until Lucia's death after fourteen years of serving as the second Pythia. And then the true line of the Pythias was born."

Allegra nodded. "I'm not sure how that would impact your perception of the power of the Pythia?"

Neptune chuckled. "The Pythias from Lydia's time would constantly thwart the deaths of hundreds of thousands of mortals. Mortals who should have died as part of the natural order of life and death. At the time, there was a philosopher who wrote his beliefs down, thoughts which merely voiced what both the gods and mortals were thinking. That soon there would be too many mortals and that they would overrun the earth and destroy everything that lay before them."

"But we didn't. The world is still turning, and we are not destroying our planet."

"That is now. There were fears in the past that the future was not looking good. But the industrialization occurred the more frequent the Pythia's predictions were. Up to a point where I too began to wonder that such a frequency must be predicting an alarming increase in under the earth activity, earthquakes, plate movement, volcanic eruptions, all meant to build to a crescendo until everything begins again."

"But you were wrong?"

"I found out all too recently in fact, that the frequency of the disaster predictions by the Pythias were easily explained, and they had nothing to do with nature taking her natural path."

"Industrialization," muttered Allegra as she thought back to Peru. She glanced at Athena who was nodding, eyebrows raised. "The more the mortals engaged in modern mining, oils, precious metals, and gems, the more the earth is disturbed."

Neptune nodded, giving her a look of pride that she wasn't sure how she should take. He had tried to kill her after all.

"INDUSTRIALIZATION, yes, but until recently I hadn't realized there was more to the link with the Pythia than I had realized."

Allegra frowned. The god seemed to be talking in circles, and she was beginning to get a headache. "I'm not sure what you mean. Industrial activity has been affecting the planet and causing increased natural disasters, which have increased the visions the oracles have been having. And you felt that the Pythia was bad for the world. And in a sense, I can understand that. And you changed your mind because you discovered this? But clearly, that was after I almost died when the *Qurux* went down."

"Yes. I'm ashamed to say that I was swayed from my original belief in the oracle to a point where I stood aside when Pythias were dying under mysterious circumstances."

"Could you have done anything about their deaths?"

"Possibly not."

"Then I don't think you are responsible unless you took action." Her unsaid words rang through around them.

Neptune nodded. "Yes. Until you, I didn't physically aid in the elimination of the Pythias. And to be honest, I didn't feel as though I would need to keep doing it. The gods know that the pythian line dies with you."

Allegra wasn't sure what to say about that, so she remained silent.

"And what is this thing you have discovered?"

"I came upon a device not too long in the past. At first, I had little idea of what the contraption did and assumed it was something the geologists or seismologist were using to measure volcanic and plate activity. But the second time I found one, I took it away. Thankfully, I didn't bring it back here with me. And to this day I regret leaving it there."

"What happened?"

"I left it deep within the Kueishan Dao, planning to find the best person to tell me what it was. But I took too long not understanding what the device was. It exploded, causing an eruption in Taiwan."

"I remember that. It was before my time. Aurelia was still the oracle then. Mara mentioned that she took it really hard because she got the prediction wrong."

"She didn't get it wrong. When a god intervenes in an event, their activity, whether it exacerbates or eliminates the threat, cannot be seen by the seer, no matter how powerful."

"So your involvement changed the prediction which is why Aurelia got the location wrong. And this device, if you found one over twenty years ago and it went off, why didn't you do something about it?"

"I didn't know. Not at the time. Then, I didn't understand the device as the cause of the explosion. I merely assumed that it was the measuring device that I have seen the divers place on the seabeds. A few weeks ago, I came upon another device, and would have taken it away had it not exploded while I was looking at it."

Allegra's jaw dropped. "But...were you hurt?"

"Nothing I cannot recover from. The point is, that is when I understood that the device triggered the explosions. I admit I didn't understand, not until it was too late."

"But there were no disasters of that nature in the last month," said Allegra wondering if she'd missed something.

"No there wasn't. Because the device I'd come across must have been some form of a test, not at all meaning to destroy anything. It was on a rocky seabed, no fault lines in the vicinity."

"So whoever these people were, they were testing the device?"

"And I discovered more. I waited for them to come to recover the device and lingered nearby. Their conversation confirmed that the event had been a test. Something about a malfunctioning mechanism that hadn't gone off in Peru."

"Peru?"

"That's a few too many coincidences for Peru," muttered Allegra but Neptune wasn't listening.

He was already halfway to the edge of the floor when he looked over his shoulder. "I must show you this device."

"And what if it exploded while the Pythia is 'looking' at it," asked Athena, her eyes dark as she followed after Allegra.

"It won't. I've learned a few things about these devices. There is a timer fixed to the side, and I believe it is counting down the hours."

"And how long do we have left?"

"As of this moment, five hours."

"That puts the tsunami at just after midday which matched what you described as the height of the sun."

Allegra nodded, and the trio rushed after Neptune who swam ahead, leading them back in the direction they'd come. The god paused and faced them, raising a hand to wave it over them as though casting a blessing upon them.

"That's to ensure you are able to breathe for the duration of the journey."

Without another word, the enigmatic god turned and swam off, headed north toward a rift on the seabed where he drew to a stop.

"We have to enter the rift valley," he said, waving them inside.

It didn't take long before Allegra was staring at the device which resembled a bomb that one would find in a fighter jet. It was long and resembled a giant cylinder, and a timer blinked on the side, now indicating five hours and ten minutes.

"What can we do with it? Is there somewhere we can take it?"

"I've arranged to have it disarmed."

"And the island will be safe? No tsunami?"

Neptune shook his head. "No tsunami, but we need to find and eliminate the person responsible." Then the god paused. "What did you mean about Peru?"

Allegra shrugged. "Someone we know popped up in Peru and we wondered how he got there before us."

"Is this person a friend or a foe?"

"Definitely a foe. From what I know he's been killing Pythias for centuries."

Neptune's face darkened, his muscles bulging and for a moment Allegra believed the god was going to kill her. Even Athena was worried because when Allegra sensed someone at her side, she found the demigod very close.

"This all makes far too much sense," Neptune bellowed.

Allegra shook her head. "Let's make sense of this in a minute. First, can we get rid of that thing?" she asked pointing at the device.

Neptune nodded and swam to the device. He grabbed it and returned, pausing at Xales' side. "Return to the grotto. I do not want you to return to the island with the Pythia just yet, there are a few things we need to discuss first."

"Yes. Then it will all make sense to us...we got that," Allegra said, glaring at the device.

Neptune let out a bellowing laugh and swam off.

CHAPTER 31

*A*llegra stared at the god Neptune, her eyes wide as her heart thudded hard against her ribs.

They were sitting in the main dining room of Allegra's resort apartment, doors closed and drapes shut to ensure their privacy. Xales was patrolling the perimeter outside the property to ensure the safety of both Allegra and Neptune in his human, and far more fragile—though exceeding attractive—form.

He stood in the apartment, his height and bulging muscles overshadowing even Xales. Long dark blonde hair hung past his shoulders in locks that would look equally attractive in or out of the water.

Unlike his previous attire, the god now wore a pair of dark blue jeans, a pale blue shirt, and a pair of leather loafers, looking the epitome of a wealthy tourist. He even had a pair of dark sunglasses tucked into his top pocket.

Allegra had been forced to refocus her attention as the god had explained his suspicions on the possible connection that Langcourt could have to the Qusqu vision and then to the vision of the Bali disaster.

Which made perfect sense given that even Allegra had questioned the man's presence in Qusqu before she'd even arrived there. There were no moles in FAPA. Langcourt had simply gotten there first, and drawn Allegra to him.

Whatever the man had intended though had been thwarted by the additional activities of General Qhapaq and his strange sect. Likely why Langcourt had disappeared into thin air. The disaster had been averted not because the general had failed to complete his ritual, but because Langcourt had fled the city.

Adding that to the existence of the same machine more than twenty years ago when Aurelia had a vision of the Jipangu eruption, and Allegra was mostly convinced. "Do you really think Langcourt set me up?"

Neptune shifted in his chair and tapped the surface of the teak table. "The discovery of that device here in Bali, just like in Keiushan Dao? I do not believe this can be a coincidence."

Allegra sat back and rubbed her forehead. "So Langcourt finds a way to activate volcanoes and maybe even earthquakes in order to draw the Pythia in. And he may be doing so for as long as these devices have been in existence." Allegra let out a weary sigh. "So you think Pompeii and Barbarina Town are safe?"

The god nodded, but Athena's jaw tightened. "I don't think we should be making any such assumptions. Not when lives are at stake."

"And what do you propose we tell Max and Marcus? Please go deep sea diving and check for a seismic trigger bomb? Or maybe we tell them everything is okay and both locations are safe even though we don't know for sure?" Allegra's last words ended a few notes higher than she'd intended.

She groaned and glanced back at Athena offering her an apologetic glance. "I'm sorry—"

Athena waved her off. "No apologies needed. This is a very high-stress situation. Someone's going to blow their top again soon. We'll be collecting a pile of 'sorrys' soon enough."

The woman did have a point. Tensions were running high, and even Neptune had lost his temper only moments ago.

"So where do we go from here?" asked Athena, her tone defeated.

"We give him some of his own medicine," Allegra bit out.

"We lure him in?"

Allegra's brow furrowed as she paused. "Okay, maybe we won't go around triggering catastrophic seismic activity, but we figure out a way to draw him to us. I want to meet the man head-on. Plus, I'd love to know what his reasons are for killing all the Pythias. The man's immortality was fed by killing innocent children. I hardly think he'd be benefiting much on that end by killing oracles."

Neptune got to his feet. "We'll likely be going around in circles for a while. Perhaps you'd better return to your teams. Bali is safe, and the tsunami has been averted. I will send my team out to scour the seabeds. I have been advised that the bombs emit a low-frequency sound that my army can hear. They will find any that are currently in position. It is how I detected the existence of the devices on both occasions."

Allegra got to her feet and began pacing. "Can we send them to Barbarian Town and Pompeii?" she said as she paused and looked over at Neptune.

The god tilted his head. "I will dispatch them as soon as I return home." Neptune bowed to Allegra. "Again, my dear Allegra, I must apologize profusely. I feel a little ill each time I think about what the world would be like had I succeeded in killing you." From the expression on his face, Allegra was certain he was being truly honest, and she found she no longer feared him, nor did she hate him.

Giving the god a smile, Allegra said, "My lord, I sincerely believe you acted in good faith. If you were ever to think that for the good of mankind, my death would help, then I'd say I understand, and I'd agree with you."

Neptune stilled as he studied Allegra, his brows creasing. "You are most gracious, Pythia Allegra."

With that, Neptune faded away, and Allegra and Athena stared at each other as the sound of gurgling water and waves faded away.

"Well, that was certainly unexpected," said Allegra staring at the empty space where Neptune had just been standing.

"You can say that again," muttered Athena. "Yes, I got to meet the god of the oceans, but I really would have preferred it to be under more pleasant circumstances."

"You can say that again," Allegra said with a wink.

CHAPTER 32

*A*llegra and Athena had arrived back home at the Pythia estate well before Max and Marcus who'd both ended up embroiled in some sort of bureaucratic upheaval.

The two women had taken the time to sleep and recuperate, and while Athena had gone off to spar in order to keep her muscles taut, Allegra disappeared into the fire-safe, this time ensuring she took food and drinks with her.

She skimmed through Lydia's codex until she saw a mention of the baby girl then skipped back a few pages.

THE WORST HAS HAPPENED. *I am with child.*

Despite every attempt at potions and oils to ensure I do not conceive again, and despite too the fact that I am nearing four decades of life, I have still become pregnant. If only the gods had heard my prayer and not allowed his seed to take, then perhaps I would not be in such danger, and nor would my child's life be in jeopardy either.

Goran has grown angry over the years. The last of the boys have left the family home. Though young they'd been placed at the homes of various senators in the Roman states. I'm most glad that they have left Goran's oppressive tutelage, but I fear that he's done his worst and succeeded too.

There is hatred in the eyes of my sons when they look upon my face. A deep-seated disgust in me, for reasons I still have not uncovered. Perhaps it has to do with the Amphora, perhaps it is because I believed Goran had no right to keep it. I wonder if I will ever know.

Will my sons return to me someday and show me the kind of love that I've yearned for? Or will time ravage me before that happens?

The babe grows within my belly, and I pray that Goran does not return before the child breathes its first. I must find a place to hide this little one. I will not give him another of my babies to turn against me.

The gods have forsaken me. And so has my husband. The love of my life. But perhaps there is no such thing as love, and perhaps what we'd had was merely a fleeting passion, because none of that affection has survived these last hard years.

I yearn for my freedom, but perhaps the only way I can get that freedom is to set my child free.

I HAVE FOUND a woman in the next village who will take the child and keep it close. My time draws near, and I fear that Goran will return too soon. I have told the women of the household to inform Goran that I have been summoned to Senator Lexius's villa.

I only hope Goran will not come looking for me.

THE PAINS WERE nothing like I'd ever experience before. I forced myself to rise and leave the villa, no sound escaping from my lips nor my feet. Perhaps the walk to the village helped ease the pain, as when I arrived, Lucia had exclaimed at how ready I was to deliver the babe. The birth was easy, something that Lucia had assured me would be the case.

I should have believed her, especially as she too is a seer. Perhaps not one with the power of the Pythia, but a seer nonetheless. I could not have found a better surrogate mother for my newborn daughter.

That the child was a girl had come as a shock to both myself and Lucia, but there was no turning back. Lucia had worn rags wrapped around her belly to mimic a pregnancy. She'd maintained the charade as we had agreed that she take the child and raise it as her own. The baby being a girl did not change the agreement, though it may have caused it to adjust itself.

Should the girl reveal the powers of the Pythia, Lucia swore that she would do everything she could to ensure the child took her rightful position. I trust Lucia implicitly and believe she will do as she has promised.

If I should die tomorrow, I will die happy knowing my precious daughter, Kassandra, is safe from him.

HE IS HOME, and I have paid dearly for my absence when he arrived. The beating was so terrible this time that I've begun to bleed profusely. The womb is a fragile thing, and I believe the injuries will ensure I do not conceive ever again. If I survive the agony, I will be happy in the knowledge that no more children will arise from our marriage bed.

I am still unsure what I have done wrong. Perhaps I have grown too old for my once-beloved husband. He has through the decades, retained his youthful looks, so much so that he still receives many an admiring glance from the prettiest of girls, unwed or not matters little. They admire him more than they should, and perhaps they feel I am too old anyway, as why would they remember that we have been married for almost thirty-five years.

Time, and Goran's dark passions have stolen my youth, but they have only infused his beauty.

ALLEGRA SAT FROZEN in shock at the words Lydia had penned.

That the woman had suffered so deeply at the hand of her husband was horrific, but her revelation, and confirmation of Neptune's recent advice, that Lydia had borne a baby girl who had grown to be the next Pythia, had stunned Allegra.

What did that really mean? That Lydia was the first of their line?

Allegra left the room, leaving behind the codex of Lydia, unable to read any further. She suspected already that Lydia's end was near and from what she'd read, Allegra was certain that the first Pythia had died at the hands of her very own husband.

The Immunis who was meant to be her protector, the one who was meant to guard her life at risk to his own.

But Goran had transformed into something despicable, and Allegra did want to know what had happened to him. The thought that Allegra's only bloodline could be traced to this awful man was something she found really hard to process.

Now, she took a deep breath as voices drifted toward her.

Her own Immunis was home, and Allegra thanked her stars that Max was nothing at all like Goran.

CHAPTER 33

*M*ax couldn't believe what Allegra was saying. Not that he didn't believe her. Just that he found it hard to wrap his head around the fact that they'd just met Neptune.

"Max you met Apollo, and you didn't appear to find it so unbelievable then," Allegra muttered, poking a fork into her salmon.

"It's not that. And besides, I met Pienius, not Apollo. He was in mortal disguise."

"It's not like Neptune was a hundred feet tall or anything. And it's not like you haven't met a god before," Allegra said, jerking a chin at Athena who responded with a glare.

"Athena? She's a demi-god. Emphasis on the demi. Means she's more mortal than god."

"How would you know, mortal?" asked Athena, her green eyes glowing for a moment, her skin rippling from human to panther, the effect a little creepy, but enough to make a point.

"Fine. I get it. Still. I may need a bit to really digest it. But in the meantime let's get back to the important issue here. Langcourt."

Allegra nodded. This was the part she wasn't at all looking forward to. "There's a bit of information about Langcourt that you all need to know."

Max's eyebrows rose. "There was more to hear?"

Allegra recounted Neptune's discovery of the bomb, and skimmed over his mention of Aurelia's incorrect prediction.

"Wait, I remember that. It was just before I arrived. Mara and Aurelia would talk about it often enough that I got the whole story only in fragments. Aurelia had a vision, and it ended up being the wrong place, and an entire island of people were killed."

"That's about the gist of it," said Allegra. "But Neptune's theory makes so much sense to me. He believes Langcourt was behind the eruptions and earthquake activity. And I agree. I think Langcourt realized that if he sets the earthquakes and natural disasters up, then the oracles will come to him. He doesn't have to go looking."

"Then all he has to do is identify her, and follow her back to where she lives. The question is, did this method work for him and for how long?"

"What you are asking is how many Pythias has he managed to kill using this method of his."

"Well, Aurelia? She died of natural causes. And then there was Cordelia, but I thought she died in the Plague of 3053?"

Max shook his head. "Aurelia mentioned it a few times. That they believed Cordelia had been deliberately infected."

"Which brings me to the next question. What disasters did Cordelia predict in the years leading to her death?"

"Hawaii," Mara's voice came from the doorway. "And Reykjavik before that." The old woman entered the dining room bearing a plate of fruits and cheeses.

"Was there anything unusual about those two visions, Mara? Can you recall anything that we can use to investigate those incidents further?"

Mara shook her head evading Allegra's eyes. "She did not share much with me. She received the visions, went with the teams, saved a lot of people in Reykjavik, although from what I recall Hawaii turned out to be a failure. She came home unhappy, moped around alot, and distrusted her ability when she received the Reykjavik prophecy. Unlike her previous visions, these two affected Cordelia deeply. But she kept the details from me."

"But you were pretty young at the time, Mara. Would you think that maybe they may not have told you everything? Just because you would have been afraid, as being so young and new to the role?" Max's question hung in the air between them, his gut insisting that the old woman wasn't sharing everything she knew. Now was not the time to hold back crucial information.

Mara's face twisted into a blend of amusement and regret. "Perhaps they did. I wouldn't have known." She turned and walked off without another word.

"Oh dear," said Athena.

Allegra glanced over at the demigod. "I do not envy you."

"Do I have to?" asked Athena staring at the empty doorway.

"What's going on?" Asked Max staring from Allegra to Athena and then back again.

Allegra chuckled. "Athena will be replacing Mara as my handmaiden."

Max glanced over at Athena, his gut twisting. "Oh dear," he said sadly, unable hold back the smile as he imagined what life for Athena was going to be like for the next year or two. Mara was a supremely hard taskmaster, and even though Athena was more or less a god, Max had a feeling the old crone would do everything in her power to make the experience supremely difficult for the demigod.

"Shut up," muttered Athena. She leaned forward and wrapped a few pieces of fruit and cheese. "Can we get back to the plan? Allegra wants to draw Langcourt in."

"I'm not sure that's a good idea."

Allegra glared at Max. "We have to do something, or else I will spend the rest of my days looking over my shoulder wondering when the bastard will pop up. And given that he doesn't die, he'll outlive me, and persecute any children that I may bring into the world. I can't sit back and wait for the next island he decides to blow up in order to draw me out."

Max sighed and rested his elbows on the table before placing his forehead in his hands. "This is so not a good idea," he said shaking his head as he stared at the table.

"But you agree we need to do it?" Allegra asked angling her head to peer down at Max's face.

He nodded and straightened, placing his hands on the table. "But let's just get one thing straight," he said, glancing from Allegra's face to Athena's both of which looked fake-innocent.

"Which is?" asked Allegra before taking a bite of cheese.

"The plan isn't the plan unless I say so. We need to be one-hundred percent sure before we move on it," Max said firmly, staring at the women as hard as he could. Then he raised an eyebrow and focused on the Pythia. "And Allegra sits this one out."

As Max tensed waiting for Allegra to fight him on it, he found himself somewhat disappointed because all she did was grab a slice of pear and smile before saying, "That was two things."

Max restrained the urge to roll his eyes. He didn't think the day would ever come that Allegra didn't test his patience.

And he hoped it never did.

CHAPTER 34

*A*llegra wasn't sure what she was supposed to do with herself. She paced the floor of her study, then wandered to the patio. The day was dreary, dark gray clouds scudded across the sky, reflecting her own frame of mind.

But the rain held, and the air was still humid enough that Allegra felt as though with every breath she swallowed a few drops of water.

She let out a sigh and paced some more, her sandaled feet making soft thugs on the stone floor.

It was easy enough to say that all she had to do was wait until a vision arrived, but there was also an element of uncertainty to it that left Allegra with an uneasy ache in her gut.

Perhaps it had more to do with the fact that she'd been so well manipulated by her adversary. Even knowing that the Pythias previous to her had also been moved around like mere chess pieces didn't make her feel any better. Langcourt had succeeded most brilliantly.

Allegra had to admit it. Arranging eruptions and quakes in order to bring the Pythia out where he could find out who she was and perhaps begin to stalk her, even track her back to wherever she lived—it all spoke to Langcourt's ability to change with the times, to use the tools around him to achieve his goals.

An intelligent opponent was always the most dangerous, and Allegra knew she had to acknowledge his smarts. Pretending they could easily outsmart the man was foolishness in the extreme.

Mara's admission that Cordelia's visions that had led her to Hawaii and then to Reykjavik had underscored Langcourt's ruthlessness. Cordelia had failed to save the villages in Hawaii and had gone to Reykjavik, her outlook despondent. Her failure had shadowed her every move, and even though she'd succeeded in saving the people in Snæland, she lived her last few months feeling as though she'd failed.

Allegra could understand that. She herself had come so close to having the very same experience, and had it not been for Neptune's discovery, Allegra would have watched the people of Bali lose thousands of lives.

And she planned to take advantage of what the god had offered. She had spent a few thoughts on Apollo, who'd helped her when she'd first become Pythia, but the god had been strangely silent all these months, and Allegra had about given up on any sort of assistance from the gods.

Her faith had been restored after Neptune's revelation, and then admission, and Allegra was all too happy to retain her position on the god's good side.

Now she had to force herself to play the waiting game, until Langcourt did whatever he did to set things into play. For now, Allegra devoted herself to two things—beginning her own entries into the Pythia Codex and brushing up on the lives of the Pythias of the past.

Although it was a difficult decision, Allegra decided to continue with Lydia's codex.

HE CHALLENGED ME, demanding to know what I had done. At first, still recovering and weak with contained bloodloss, I didn't understand.

He hit me then, his palm connecting with my cheek so hard that my neck snapped. But I dared not react, tears would merely encourage further violence as he attempted to quiet me, reluctant to bring his treatment to me to the attention of the household or the priests.

Little does he know that both the household and the priesthood were well aware of his behavior, and they'd slowly withdrawn their support of him.

My silence encouraged him to speak, and he went onto describe the encounter he'd had with the most senior of the Pythian priests who had only moments ago demanded that Goran hand over the amphora he'd taken from Atlantis, citing historical significance and it being the property of all citizenry.

I denied all knowledge which of course had been a lie. I am guilty of turning my husband in, of revealing his theft of the amphora to the senate who would have sent the priests to discuss the issue with him.

But that discussion with the senate had taken place more than ten years past, and I wonder why they'd taken so long to do something about him. Still, I have never spoken of his treatment of me. There is far too much shame in that.

Perhaps the oracles who come after me will learn from my mistakes and take more care in the choice of their life mates. I have made my request with the Pythia Council for a more strict decision-making process in the choosing of the Immunis. The ability of a male to be immune from the touch of the oracle does not necessarily make him the automatically chosen mate of the Pythia.

I know of two other males, a senator and a laborer in a neighboring villa who were immunis too, only not officially recognized. Is it but a fable that there is only one? I often wonder if perhaps there is an element of truth to this.

Goran did not take the demands lightly, announcing that he would take the amphora and leave. And his expression was particularly *strange, trancelike, and he spoke without looking at me, as though I were not there at all.*

He lives in a strange world, one he had only muttered about in passing, and as each day draws by, I have grown more and more afraid for him

And today he stood in front of me, announcing his intention to do the one thing I knew would spell the end.

I should have listened to my gut, should never have given into the ever-present desire to please my husband. I'd chosen to give him his dreams, only to have his reality taken from him. Had I caused him to lose his mind this way? To move so far apart from reality that he no longer made sense within our world.

I see before me a man who looks no older than thirty, a man who I know is no younger than fifty years of age. How can he evade the ravages of time in this way? Has he managed to delude himself into believing himself to still be the bright young man I had fallen in love with all those years ago?

And he barely even knows it, that is how far he has gone, how deeply he has become embroiled in this delusions.

ALLEGRA BLINKED, trying to squeeze the gritty feeling out of her eyes. Lydia's life had taken a turn for the worse, and as Allegra turned the page, she found nothing more. The codex of the Pythia Lydia had ended with a small entry by her successor indicating the year of her death.

Just like that, the woman who was the progenitor of the entire line of Pythias was gone.

CHAPTER 35

Akída, (Fora Islet, Canaries)

LANGCOURT PACED the floor of his office, his bald head growing hot with fury as he thought about the disaster that was the Bali earthquake. Nothing had gone as he had planned and he was confused.

For more than a century now, Langcourt had been using a sonic emitter which created vibrations within the earth, vibrations that could lead to tremors and earthquakes. But the core mechanism was outdated and prone to untimely failures. That was what Von Demme had been hired to do.

To fix the damned core mechanism.

Something he'd failed to do.

But had he failed, or had someone helped the Pythia? Given her details in advance that would allow her to destroy his bomb? Or perhaps sabotaged it on her behalf?

So he found it difficult to identify a singular person within his employ who would have understood who he was and what he'd intended to do. Even the team he'd hired in Barbarina Town to abduct the Pythia and subdue her familiar hadn't really known who they were working for.

An arrangement that had worked to Langcourt's advantage for centuries. Still, there were times when that arrangement fell apart and the men in his employ turned the tables on him.

For centuries, Langcourt's elder brother Claudius had spear-headed most of their attempts to eliminate the Pythias, leaving Severus and his younger brothers to do the dirty work. Had Claudius been in charge, it would have been Langcourt himself who would have been the one to dive to the seabeds or rappel down the sides of rift valleys in order to place the devices and activate them.

It gave Langcourt a moment of pleasure to know that his dear brother had not lived long enough to avail himself of the most modern of technologies.

Claudius had met a bloody end during the revolution in Frankia in 2799 where his father and brothers had witnessed him being relieved of his head in a long, gory, and bloody process.

As much as Langcourt had competed with his brother for their father's attention, he'd never have wished such a death upon Claudius who had survived much of the attempt and had only drawn his last breath seconds before the final incision.

His father had been most devastated, his first born having been the apple of his eye. Still, he transferred the mantle of management over to Langcourt who proved far more tactically skilled than the old man had envisioned.

In fact, before he'd been killed, Langcourt's father had given him a birthday gift he'd never have expected—a safari to South Alkebulan, to fulfill a long-standing dream to fell an elephant with a single bullet.

That trip had ended in tragedy, a day that Langcourt would never forget no matter how long he lived. Claudius' death at the hands of the Pythian assassins had been bloody and deadly, and protracted.

The deaths of his family in darkest Alkebulan had been a massacre. Lord Alderman Langcourt, the name by which Langcourt and his family had gone by for the last 200 years since Claudius' death, and his remaining sons must have stepped on the wrong toes when they'd entered the country in search of their prey.

Elephant hunting was well controlled by the chiefs within each region of Greater Alkebulan, and perhaps more so by the warrior tribes of the Southern half of the continent.

The chief of the local Zulu tribe, a terrifyingly violent people, who had welcomed the family Langcourt with a meal and performance that had given the young Severus chills. His father though had seemed unimpressed, almost dismissive as though he'd seen it all before and the sight had bored him.

As THRILLED as Severus was with this incomparable gift his father had given him, the son did experience a moment or two or trepidation. Perhaps an odd pulsing in the gut that seemed to warn him that some of one's wishes are not meant to be realized.

Their arrival at the port had proved most inauspicious, the ship being tossed about on the seas and almost smashed to smithereens on the rocky approach.

They'd docked at last, to the relief of the brothers who had all experienced an extended bout of seasickness. The elder Langcourt though had appeared immune to such things, standing at the port bow, staring off at the coastline, experiencing what Severus could only describe as an intense melancholy.

The two younger sons, Aquila and Julius, had been on their best behavior, though Severus had to wonder if the pair had somehow contributed to whatever had motivated the massacre.

At the port town, their overnight stay before the trek to the jungle had been filled with drunken carousing in the town, along with an incident with a pair of girls who worked at a local hotel. Severus had rounded-up the boys—who had remained boys in his mind even though centuries had passed—and paid the tavern master off.

The girls he could do nothing about and was only glad to have the caravan head out the next morning. The drive to the jungle's borders had taken two days of difficult travel over rough terrain and sandy roads peppered with potholes that made for a journey far more nauseating than their recent sea journey.

Though surrounded by trees edged with thorns, and dense bushes, the family had felt safe enough, with the protection of the local tour company and two law officers. Their trip had proceeded much to Severus' expectation—in that the tracking and shooting of his prized elephant had much resembled what his imagination had created for him over the years.

The result had been a grand kill, one which the tusks would have brought them an astronomical fee. But they'd never gotten to sell it. Not long after the elephant had gone down, and the photograph taken the photo of the four men and their kill, they'd left the site, leaving the tour company to take care of the carcass. The only thing they took with them were the tusks.

Likely the reason the Langcourts had met their end. They'd barely driven a mile away from the site of their kill, when they were beset by a band of warriors who emerged from the trees, dark-skinned, straight-backed, bare-chested. They'd stood in the path of the vehicles, forcing them to come to a stop, then gathered in a large circle, demanding the family along with their guides alight from their vehicles.

Severus had welcomed the opportunity to engage with a local tribe, his interest in anthropologic studying being quite serious at the time. But his desire to understand these people had gone unquenched as the leader in his headdress of feathers and his skirt of skins marched toward his father, raising his spear and slamming it upon his cow-hide shield.

With the guides urging them to remain calm, the Langcourts obeyed the instructions to walk deeper into the jungle, even while aware that the encroaching darkness could be filled with dangerous animals. They'd walked for what had seemed to be hours, though the truth of it Severus would never really know.

At last, they'd come to what appeared to be the border of a cemetery where the men were instructed to dig their own graves. Stunned, though with little choice, they obeyed, well aware that the tour guide and their translator had been taken away. Whether or not the pair would survive, Severus didn't know and didn't expect to ever find out.

With the graves dug, the chief began to sing out, and a car drove up moments later, one filled with rocks and driven by two masked men. Mildly curious as to the need for masks when the family was no doubt going to be killed, Severus considered who these strangers could be. Certainly not tribal from their clothing, but with the masks, he could not be sure. The men, along with half a dozen warriors had proceeded to offload the rocks.

It was only later that Severus understood the reasons for the rocks. With little warning, the warriors let loose a round of spears, then a second volley followed, the attackers uncaring of how many spears protruded from their bodies.

The family were all still alive after the brutal attack, and as he lay there on the handpicked soil, he watched as one of the masked men walked along, pouring a liquid first upon his brothers and then his father. The old man struggled, perhaps using the last of his strength, and managed to topple the jar from the masked man's hand.

Though furious, the man retrieved the jar and emptied what had remained onto Severus, who'd been unable to resist and had shown not an iota of courage. The disappointment was clear in his father's eyes.

A while later, Severus listened to the cries of his family, long after their bodies had been thrown into their respective graves, and then covered in alternating layers of soil and stones.

Lying there, time passed excruciating slowly, the pressure of the soil and stones seeming to flatten Severus hour by hour, day by day. He'd taken to counting the days by listening to the birds calling at sunrise, and the passing of an elephant herd as they made their way to and from every day.

In the end, Severus had kept track of the passing of time using nature's cycles. At day ninety-seven, Julius had ceased his calling. Day one-hundred-and-sixteen marked the passing of Aquila.

The elder Langcourt breathed his last at day two-hundred-and-forty-one, much of that time spent voicing his disappointment in his second son, praising the successes of Claudius and claiming Severus was far too much like his mother.

Those ravings soon turned nonsensical and faded away leaving the disappointing coward of a second son to count down until nine-hundred-and-twenty days. After that he'd lost count, growing more and more delirious as time passed.

His release from his stone and sand prison had come as a surprise, a complete accident by the looks of it. A group of people passed by one night, the language they spoke making Severus guess at Frankia, which in the end had been the irony of all ironies.

He'd called out and kept calling until they'd heard his voice and followed it to the grave. The good samaritans had proceeded to dig a filthy, emaciated Severus out of his grave, and had expressed horror at his predicament. They had helped him clean up, given him food, water, and a change of clothing. They had even provided Severus with weapons and a vehicle, although those were not due to their kind generosity.

Severus left the secluded spot, along with the bodies of the three hunters, stripped naked and laid bare for the circling vultures, and drove himself back to the port where he discovered, much to his horror, that he'd been buried in that pit for fourteen years.

Which he'd only found out because he'd gone looking for the tour company who'd sold his family out, only to find they closed for business eight years prior.

In a daze, Severus boarded a vessel up the west coast of Alkebulan to the hideaway island the family had held for almost three millennia.

Home to Akída.

LANGCOURT BLINKED as he became aware again of his study and of where he was, the memories of being buried for so many years seeming to overwhelm him for a moment. But it didn't take long for him to return to his train of thought, and to his suspicion that someone who worked for him was responsible.

His fingers curled into a fist and before he knew it, he'd punched a hole in the wall, cracking the paintwork and sending a shower of plaster and pale yellow flakes to the lush Anatolian carpet.

Langcourt considered that for a moment, his mind flickering with thoughts of possible traitors within his midst. He'd been most careful through his long lifetime, cultivating relationships with people, mutually beneficial partnerships with only one caveat. Very few of his contacts knew who he was, and almost none had ever set eyes on Langcourt's face.

Seconds later, the door was flung open, a breathless Roquefort skidding to a stop on the threshold, staring around the room, eyes rounded.

Roquefort.

The now ruined man—skin on his face tight and shriveled, half his hair burnt off—had been with Langcourt for most of his mission to kill the Pythia Allegra. The man who'd once attempted to counsel Langcourt against such a murderous choice.

"Was it you?" Severus hollered, anger darkening his vision as he rounded on the man who'd stepped into the study and approached his master, concern in his gaze as he stared at the wall and then at Langcourt's bloodied first.

"Me, my lord?" Roquefort asked, frowning now.

Lancourt lashed out, fingers encircling the man's throat. "I want the truth. Was it you who gave them the information?"

"No, sir. I swear it was not me."

Langcourt shook the man hard then raised him off the ground, yelling, "I want the truth. Did you or did you not tip off the Pythia or her team?"

The man struggled in Langcourt's grip. "No," he squawked, his eyes bulging as he tried to shake his head. Roquefort gasped, but Langcourt didn't release the pressure.

But the man's terror was real as Lancourt stared into Roquefort's eyes. But even as he came to the conclusion that his assistant was loyal and true, Langcourt heard the clicking beneath his fingers and watched as the man's eyes rolled and slumped heavily against the death-grip.

Langcourt let go of the man and watched him crumple to the floor, lifeless.

He'd killed Roquefort, but the man had been innocent.

Taking a deep breath, Langcourt strode from the room, a pulsing of regret of the loss of the man. It meant the menial tasks would have to shift back to Langcourt himself.

At least until he could obtain a suitable replacement.

CHAPTER 36

*T*he land beneath Allegra's feet shook so violently that she staggered, unable to keep upright. She lost her footing, and fell to the ground so hard she was surprised that she hadn't broken anything.

There she sat and stared around her, both terrified and aware, knowing what this dream meant. Wherever this place was, Langcourt was playing his game, drawing her to him. And now all she had to do was identify where in the world she was.

She forced herself to get to her feet and scanned her surroundings. Straight ahead of her and about two miles down the hill was a narrow channel, and across a low lying strip of land. To the right, all Allegra saw was ocean in the distance, and to the left, the river widened to a bay that appeared almost as a lake, then disappeared in the distance.

A few yards to Allegra's left, was a chasm that emitted a rush of smoke, a rift that began to widen the longer the ground shook. Below the hill and along the river's edge, was a small city, but unless Allegra went down into the streets, there was little chance of her identifying any landmarks. And two miles was a long way away, even if she tried to get there on foot.

Even so, the entire town had begun to shift, undulating at the surface as the land began to shake, as though the very ground had turned to liquid. Allegra gasped, knowing the city itself had little chance.

As she struggled to stay upright, a group of people rushed past, racing to get down the hillside to safety, discarding bicycles and prams as they fled, while the chasm ripped open and widened, following in their wake.

She wanted to yell at them to stop, to stay away from the city, to keep away from the chasm, but it was too late.

Allegra cried, holding back a rush of tears as she looked away. Swallowing hard, she spotted one of the prams and staggered over to it, then crouched beside it, hoping there would be something the family had left behind. All she could see was a company logo, LusiMoro, but nothing else.

Despondent, Allegra got to her feet, unable to look away from the seaside where the city had now vanished into the earth, an open chasm the only thing left, the river surging into its depths like a waterfall.

And she felt the vision beginning to fade.

ALLEGRA LIFTED HER HEAD, feeling the tight muscles in her neck complain loudly. Perspiration covered her skin and she was glad she'd been lying to the side of Lydia's Codex.

Blinking, Allegra glanced down at the words that had come straight from the woman's heart, feeling again a pang of pain for the suffering the woman had gone through.

Allegra stared down at the words, a paragraph of sadness in which the Pythia Lydia described her longing for her sons, boys who she'd loved and lost before they had even reached their fifth year.

She read the the names of the little boys, all siblings for the hidden Pythia Kassandra.

Then Allegra shook her head and got to her feet. There was

work to be done. And knowing Langcourt, Allegra didn't have much time.

She prayed fervently that the name on the pram would help them identify the town. Prayed for something, anything that would help them save those innocent people.

And end this war with Langcourt once and for all.

CHAPTER 37

*A*llegra was standing on the stone balcony overlooking the valley below the Pythia's estate, waiting as Max prepared his plan.

She held back a smile as Athena glanced at her and rolled her eyes. Max was rather serious about the whole plan, but Allegra supposed she would humor him.

At last, Max straightened, and looked up at the two woman, a scowl ruining his beautiful features.

Allegra knew they made a strange picture, sitting on the balcony in dark glasses and brightly colored sundresses, the sun blazing down on them. They looked like the most unlikely two women to be involved in a mission to eliminate a notorious killer.

To make matters worse, both women were sipping an unusual drink which the Pythian delegate from Roma had delivered, a bright blue concoction that claimed to be a prosecco.

Interesting, even if a little too sweet for Allegra's taste. Athena, on the other hand, had knocked back a few already, and if Allegra didn't watch her ,the demigod would be wasted in no time.

Max cleared his throat. "So LusiMoro is a company that manufactures baby goods, it's based in Lusitania, which helps us narrow down the country at least.

"What about the description of the bay and the narrow channel with the ocean on the right?" asked Allegra, shaking her foot as anxiety began to built slowly.

"That description has fit only one town that sits in an area known for seismic activity."

Max handed Allegra a map, and she nodded. "Lusitania, Gallaeci? That definitely looks like the land mass. I was on a higher elevation though, so that would be around here?" Allegra pointed to an area where the green graduated from dark to light to indicate elevation. She tapped the blue label of Nerthallasus. "This would be the ocean I saw."

Athena downed the remainder of her blue bubbles and clapped her hands, rising to her feet. "So it's off to Gallaeci?"

Max pursed his lips and then nodded. He glanced over at Allegra. "God of the Oceans? You got a number for him?"

Athena choked with laughter while Allegra rolled her eyes. "No. I don't believe satellite phones work well when submerged." She smirked, then said, "But I think I may have a way to contact him."

"Going for a swim?" asked Max, giving Allegra a suggestive look.

Athena groaned and walked off the balcony. "That's my cue. You two need to get a room. I can't believe I'd prefer Mara's company right now." And with that the demigod disappeared into the villa.

Max chuckled. "It's so easy to poke fun at her."

"You shouldn't take advantage of it. The jaguar does have a dangerous set of claws. And teeth." Allegra got to her feet, leaving her glass on the table before heading inside. On the threshold, she looked back at Max. "I won't be long. How much time do you think we have?"

"I don't think time really matters. Langcourt has set everything in motion already, or you wouldn't have had the dream. But the point was to draw you out—which he would have catered for if he plans on lying in wait for you—so whether we get there now or in three days it doesn't matter."

"What if it does matter, and he initiates the earthquake if I don't get there in time?"

Max didn't reply, and Allegra left him to his silence. She passed Les on her way to the lake, the woman waving at her from her archery practice. Over the last few weeks, Les had progressed through the training, proving both to Max and herself that her training in the military had remained within her core.

The team had left her to it, Max and Athena observing the woman's progress every so often. Allegra had suggested they take her along on the mission to Bali, but Max had insisted she wasn't ready.

Now, Allegra didn't bring it up with Max, deciding he would bring Les on when he was good and ready.

Allegra returned Les's greeting and made her way beyond the villa and down to the lake, hoping that her hunch would pay off.

Water was water, whether salt or fresh. Hopefully Neptune didn't have a problem with that.

CHAPTER 38

The team arrived in Lusitania in the early morning, and was greeted by a squall, the sky gray and dull, and hammering the earth with intermittent storms.

"Perfect weather for climbing unfamiliar mountains," muttered Athena as she laced up her boots while everyone grabbed their bags to get off the plane.

Allegra barely paid her any attention, her mind already focused on what she would find up on the hillside.

They'd decided to check the site first, to be sure Lusitania was the place they were looking for. Then the plan was to head into the town and check into a local hotel.

Max had hired a small Jeep which he'd elected to drive, his second grab at maintaining some form of control of the events that were soon to pass.

Xales remained at Allegra's side all the way up the mountain, his almost visible but not quite form giving her comfort.

At the peak of the mountain, the team alighted from the vehicle and stared out at the vista, Athena spinning around and giving a low whistle. "This is impressive."

Allegra nodded. "And it's the place in my vision," she said, her tone low and serious. She was not in the mood to be impressed, not when the whole place was likely to be swallowed up by a giant rift in the earth.

Max looked over at Allegra and gave her a comforting smile "Ready to head into the town?"

Allegra didn't reply. She hurried to the vehicle and jumped inside, not in the mood for smalltalk either.

Max and Athena seemed to understand, though both kept throwing Allegra glances filled with concern.

They drove into the city, the quaint cobblestone streets, harking back to an era where horses and carriages were the norm.

Their hotel turned out to be a small castle with influences from the Moors, the Spanish, and the Persians, all mixed up with a good dose of Roman. It made for quite the Byzantine feel and Allegra found she quite enjoyed it. If she managed to save the town she'd happily return to enjoy the sights.

As they dropped their bags on the floor of their two bedroomed suite, the air began to shimmer and the shape of a man appeared. Max drew his weapon in one move, but Allegra waved him down.

Max relaxed, but he didn't holster his weapon, not until Allegra introduced him to Neptune.

The god did not look happy and before he opened his mouth, Allegra found her heart tightening.

"I'm afraid I could find no trace of the devices, my lady. My teams have been searching along the western shores of this land mass, but they've found nothing."

"Perhaps he's hidden it on land somewhere," suggested Athena, eyeing Neptune with more than a little admiration.

But Allegra barely paid attention to the demigod's behavior. Her words were far more important.

Allegra nodded slowly. "What if Langcourt set the device down in a chasm from a previous eruption?"

"That could be it," said Max. "Lusitania suffered a terrible earthquake about two hundred and fifty years ago. The quake resulted in a tsunami that destroyed much of the coastline including the seaside towns of Espania and Murakush and caused a number of smaller tidal waves as far away as East Amazonia and Eire."

"Any chasms?"

"In the middle of the city, reported to be as wide as five yards in some places."

"That would be the most likely place. We just need to figure out how to get down there to dismantle the thing."

"Leave that to me," said Neptune before he disappeared.

Max cocked an eyebrow. "Personable fellow," he muttered as he stared at the empty spot where Neptune had been standing.

Allegra let out a sigh and said, "So, I think it's time to decide what we do next. Time I walked around, let Langcourt know I'm here and waiting."

"I didn't realize we were going to put you in harm's way," said Max, his tone dangerous.

Allegra shrugged. "Xales is with me. I doubt he'll let any harm come to me."

"The way he prevents you from being abducted by Langcourt's goons even when you had a security team surrounding you twenty-four-seven?" Max's face was dark now, a vein throbbing in his temple.

Allegra let out a low grunt. "Max, we don't have time for this. Even if Neptune succeeds, I can't just sit around here and wait for Langcourt to find me. We need to be the ones in control for once. We lure him in on our terms."

Allegra stared around her, noticing that Xales had materialized as she'd been speaking. He nodded, offering his approval.

Though Max looked unhappy, he also appeared to be acquiescing, much to Allegra's relief.

Max nodded. "I don't like it, but you may be right." He

reached into the pocket of his jacket and withdrew a black band, handing it over to Allegra. "It's a tracker."

"Very feminine," Allegra said as she hooked the fabric covered elastic band around her ponytail.

"Lots of female agents in the field. And a few males would make use of it too." Max smiled, and Allegra returned it with her own grin.

Taking a deep breath, Allegra said, "So, I head out and you guys cover me?"

Allegra received a chorus of nods and relaxed, though only a fraction. "If he takes me, you won't stop him."

"I don't thin—"

"That wasn't a question, Athena," said Allegra calmly.

Athena clamped her mouth shut, her jaw tightening. Max held up a hand and chuckled. "Right, we head out, keep our eyes open. I'll keep as far back as I can. Athena?"

"I'll use my glamor. I don't use it often. Makes me queasy. But I don't think a large jaguar roaming the streets of Lusitania will go down well."

Allegra laughed, the action allowing her to relax for a the first time since they'd landed.

She rummaged in her suitcase for her large hat and sunglasses, then she gave the team a nod and crossed the room to open the door. Xales had disappeared but Allegra sensed his presence at her side as she left the hotel room and strolled outside. She used the hat and glasses even though they would conceal her identity.

Langcourt would already know it was her; he was already watching, that much she could guarantee.

CHAPTER 39

*L*angcourt let out a soft laugh, careful to not appear deranged to the woman in blue who sat at the table next to him.

She'd been sending him pointed glances for the last hour, and he wasn't sure if she was watching him because he was paying far too much attention to the coffee shop across the street or because she was interested in him.

He found the latter hard to believe.

Focusing on the Pythia, Langcourt was relieved that she'd come almost immediately. He'd set things in motion, after he'd arranged for Roquefort's body to be removed from his study, of course. And now it was all coming neatly together.

The FAPA commander was with her, which he'd expected. But so was the police chief from Qusqu. Now that was something Langcourt had not expected.

Either way, none of them mattered.

Langcourt got to his feet and left his table, ignoring the infinite coffee and cake he'd left behind. Outside, he paused to push his own white wide-brimmed hat on his bald head, then crossed the street.

It appeared that the Pythia was alone and without her usual backup team, Langcourt had little idea if he was wrong.

Again, it didn't matter.

He entered the coffee shop, and headed to the Pythia's table where he took a seat directly opposite her, his smile wide.

His smile grew wider when she winced, as though he'd slapped her.

"I see I have your undivided attention at last."

The Pythia smiled, and Langcourt found it strange how pleasant she seemed. If she was anyone else, he may even have liked her.

He knew he'd felt quite bad after he'd whipped her raw in Londonium the first time they'd met. He'd wondered if perhaps he'd been a little too harsh with her.

Either way that was in the past.

Today, he would grab hold of the future with both hands.

"Are you ready to leave?"

"Yes, I'm heading back to my hotel."

"I don't believe you are," Langcourt said as he got to his feet. As he looked out the window an executive cab drew up to the sidewalk and Langcourt smiled. "Here is our ride. Perhaps you will come without creating a fuss?"

He'd spoke the words as though they were a suggestion, but the steel in his tone said otherwise.

And from the way the Pythia got to her feet, Langcourt knew then that he'd already won.

Now to take his prize home.

ALLEGRA HAD GONE WITH LANGCOURT, refusing to make a scene, as he'd said. Besides, this was the place after all.

His cab had driven them to the docks where Langcourt had led Allegra along the pier to a row of pleasure cruisers where they boarded a vessel called The Lady L. Allegra had paused at the sight of the name, something bugging her that was just out of reach.

Langcourt had urged her forward, muttering something about his mother in explanation for the name.

Once inside, Langcourt handed her a suitcase. "Remove all your clothing. I am quite confident that you have some form of tracking device on your person so I've taken precautions."

Allegra grabbed the bag and entered the main stateroom that the man had indicated with a careless wave.

She changed into a long blue dress, and returned his suitcase. Langcourt took the bag and smirked. "Hair accessories as well if you don't mind."

Allegra had no choice but to comply, following which Langcourt left her alone, the sound of his low laughter echoing behind him.

In the trip across the ocean, the only consolation for Allegra was Xales' constant comforting presence.

CHAPTER 40

Max paced the floor of the hotel room, regretting having agreed to let Allegra be bait. He'd relied on the tracker for the security he'd needed, believed he'd be able to maintain some kind of link with Allegra. That would keep her safe.

But the tracker had died. At first, Max assumed the indicator panel was faulty. But very soon, he realized the the problem lay with the tracker itself.

After slamming the device down onto the center of his palm at least a dozen times, Athena had yelled at him to stop. "You are going to break the damn thing," she said scowling at him.

Max had relented, having come to terms with the fact that the device was not going to help him track Allegra.

"Now what?" Athena asked as she paced in front of the bedroom window.

Max shook his head. "I'm not exactly sure. Who knows where we go from here?"

"Max, I think you are forgetting your agent skills," replied Athena giving him a disgusted look. "This is the reason why matters of the heart should not coincide with matters of business."

Max took long breath. "I'm just worried. I had it all planned. And now those plans have gone up in smoke. He lured her here. She came. And now he has her, and I did nothing to stop him."

"If you are finished with your pity party, maybe you can start checking the airports while I check the docks. There are likely only two ways he would've gotten her out of the country. And I don't see him going inland."

Max nodded. "You're right. I'll make a few calls, get some eyeballs on those flight paths."

The next few moments were spent scanning flight departures and sealanes in the hopes of finding what Langcourt had used to escape the country.

Once the searches were completed, Max began to pace again. Then he paused and looked at Athena. "Do you think Neptune would be able to help us?"

"I don't see why not. We are asking him to help if we are looking at a water getaway."

Max smiled. "Something tells me that Langcourt hasn't gone far. He had this planned. I doubt that he would've taken her too far."

"So what do we know about him? Is there something about him, perhaps in his past that we could use to make a guess as to where he really is right now?"

Max pulled out his phone. "I do have some details, mostly information that we have been able to pull from Aurelia's diary." Max scanned his phone for a few minutes then looked up at Athena with a huge grin on his face. "I think I have it. There is a property on an island not far from here that has been held under a convoluted array of subsidiary companies. It has belonged to the same company, and by virtue that, the same owners for the better part of the last thousand years."

"I think we may have our guy," said Athena bouncing on her

feet. "I'm not sure how we are supposed to alert Neptune though."

"It likely doesn't matter. We have the coordinates of the island. I'll have a boat chartered in no time."

Athena smiled as Max proceeded to arrange a small craft, reporting his success within minutes. The pair gathered their possessions, including Allegra's, and checked out of the hotel, heading straight for the docks.

Max breathed his first sigh of relief when he was on the water speeding toward the island of Akída.

Langcourt better hope he was already dead before Max got to him. Because when Max got there, he was going to make the man suffer.

CHAPTER 41

*F*or the most part, Langcourt had been the perfect gentleman, even as he'd guided Allegra off the boat and toward the jetty.

The man, for all his deadly activities, did not cut an imposing or frightening figure. Her impressions from when she'd met Langcourt for the first time in Brittania a few months ago remained unchanged.

His scowling countenance along with his unimposing height made for a man easy to forget. Still, his actions spoke louder than his looks, considering the number of corpses he'd left in his wake over the centuries.

She'd watched the approach to the island, and marveled at the beauty of the place, so secluded, with the feel of being alone in the middle of the ocean.

Langcourt didn't say much, but Allegra guessed from the direction of the sun, that they'd traveled south-west toward the Canaries, just off the west coast of Alkebulan.

They were met at the docks by an old man, so wrinkled that it was hard to tell his race, his skin tanned to a leathery-brown. He could have been from anywhere in the world.

Attempting to identify exactly which island she was on was going to be harder than she'd thought. The brush of fur beside her, told her Xales was right there with her. For the longest time since Langcourt had taken her from the coffee shop in Lusitania, Allegra had felt something niggling at the back of her mind, but she'd been unable to put a finger on it.

At first, she'd wondered if it was because she was now on her own with no backup and no sign of Max or Athena. But it wasn't that. It had much more to do with Langcourt himself.

And although she was so tempted to talk it over with Xales, she did not dare in case the man realized that her familiar was with her constantly.

As they rode the narrow dirt track over the undulating hills toward a villa in the distance, Allegra studied the island. Apart from the enormous residence on the hill, the land was half-vineyard, half-farmland.

And yet no sign of homes for tenants or farmworkers who worked the land. How strange.

As they topped a low hill, Allegra caught a flash of white in the distance, her eyes widening at the sight of the temple grounds. Even from this distance she identified the carvings and the design of the parthenon which announced the temple as belonging to the goddesses Themis, Gaia, and Phoebe.

Now why in Hades would Langcourt give a flying drachma about the trio of goddesses who were the patrons of the oracles from a time so ancient that most people had forgotten they'd been worshiped by the first seers, the Sybils? Even before Apollo was granted patronage of the Pythias.

The further she went on this journey with her captor, the more confusing things became.

Langcourt sat up front beside the old man, and as Allegra studied him, she began to notice a few more things about the man that hadn't impacted her when she'd run into him, likely because he'd abducted her.

His skin was wrinkled and dry, and bore the look of an old man. And now, with him sitting beside the wrinkled old prune of a driver it was so easy to see.

Langcourt's immortality was fading fast, and Allegra had to wonder if it had to do with the fact that he may not have performed the relevant sacrifices in order to maintain his longevity.

She shuddered at the thought of sacrifices, recalling the face of the little blue-eyed child, who'd been killed and drained of his blood while Allegra had been forced to watch. The Society of Hermes had perished soon after that particular sacrifice, thanks in part to Allegra uncovering its existence.

But Allegra also recalled her words to Langcourt, words filled with such hatred and passion, spoken as though she'd seen his future. Which had been a lie. More like wishful thinking. She'd wanted to see him suffer for what he'd done to the little child, but seeing the man now, she grasped a meagre understanding of his motives.

Any man staring death in the face after hundred of years alive, would likely do everything in his power to remain breathing—even kill innocent children.

Mortals were capable of the worst atrocities. Not that the gods were all that innocent.

Allegra took a slow breath as she stilled the rapid beating of her heart. The small vehicle ascended the hillside, the engine grunting as it struggled toward the entrance to the villa. Lined with two rows of tall firs, the long dirt avenue was bracketed by gardens filled with fruit trees of every species Allegra knew of, and some she was unfamiliar with.

She shook her head, pulling her attention from the scenery to focus on her captor, her nemesis, the man who'd obliterated her bloodline.

She could not afford to be distracted.

INSIDE THE VILLA, Langcourt led Allegra to a small study, the walls lined with books. None of the leather spines bore titles, which added to the mystery of the place.

Oddly enough, the books resembled the Pythias Codices, which again gave Allegra that strange feeling, as though she was missing something.

Langcourt spoke just then, pulling her from her thoughts. "I must thank you, my lady," he said, his tone bearing an edge of mockery at her title. "You have made this process infinitely easier than I had anticipated."

Allegra lifted an eyebrow. "It isn't as though you have given me much of a choice, sir." Her own tone was cutting, though not a fitting response to his condescension.

Langcourt let out a loud laugh, the sound grating on Allegra's ears.

"I suggest you get on with whatever it is you plan to do. I'm not a patient woman."

Langcourt snorted. "Barely a Pythia for five moons and you already bear the arrogance of your line."

"A line that has been decimated thanks to you," Allegra spat, her eyes flashing with fury. In that moment, she wished she had the power to blast a stream of flames at the man and incinerate him on the spot. Then she amended her fantasy; he didn't deserve such a quick death.

"You, my dear Allegra, I had almost missed. I'd been certain we had found all of you, but it's clear that somewhere along the line the oracles have managed to thwart our mission."

"Our mission? Why aren't you taking all the credit for the serial murders of my family?"

Langcourt shrugged. "First, it is not murder when one is avenging oneself. And second, I have not been alone in my crusade. My father and brothers have been part of the mission for all these years."

Allegra blinked. "The men on the safari," she whispered. "Right. He was your father."

"How do you know about that?" he growled.

Allegra smirked. "You touched me. I had a vision. Simple enough."

Langcourt's jaw tightened as he considered her words, then he laughed, dismissing her with a flick of his fingers. "It matters little now. You will see your end very soon. And then I will be free of you and your family."

"What do you have against us?"

Langourt glanced at Allegra, as though startled at her voice.

"This crusade you and your family have carried out over the centuries—"

"Millenia. Three to be specific." Langcourt smirked as though proud of the length of time in which he'd spent killing people in cold blood.

Allegra startled at the revelation. Three thousand years. About as long as the Pythia line had existed.

Was this man really three millennia old? Allegra shook her head. "You're looking a little worse for wear. Not killing any innocent children in recent times?" Allegra asked, fury filling her to the brim.

Langcourt laughed. "That was an unfortunate attempt at holding the effects of time at bay. A purely temporary fix."

"So you created this Society of Hermes as a front to perform those rituals? To consume the fresh blood so it would boost your fading immortality?" Allegra asked, attempting to keep him talking. And perhaps a little curious as to how the man's mind worked.

Langcourt nodded, tapping his finger on his desk. "Yes, but it didn't work as planned."

"How did you become immortal? Perhaps you ought to chase down your origins and figure out a less deadly way to extend your...

life." Allegra had wanted to throw a few words at the man, pathetic and sorry accounting for only two of her options. But she'd bitten the words back and opted for civility. She needed information. Information would be her weapon to bring Langcourt to justice.

Langcourt sighed deeply and got to his feet. "Perhaps I ought to show you. There is little need for secrecy now that I have you where I want you. If all goes to plan, I may not even need to kill you."

Allegra shook her head. "You were about to tell me how you became immortal," Allegra probed again.

Langcourt was already walking out the door. "I was born this way," he said as he led her down the hall.

The villa was a warren of corridors within which Allegra had lost her way within bare minutes. Langcourt led her toward the center of the residence and then into what appeared to be a small room.

It turned out to be a stairwell that led deep within the island, the stairs made of stone and carved directly into the rocky center of the mountain.

A cool breeze caressed Allegra's skin, and the further she descended, the more moist the air became. They were nearing water, of that much she was certain. Perhaps there was a second exit within this hidden chamber; Allegra would have to keep her eyes wary as she descended.

The stairs ended, and led Allegra into a large grotto at the center of which was a structure that struck Allegra as terribly familiar.

Circular patterns were carved around the stone floor of the grotto, each smaller than the next until they ended at the steps to the central, dome-ceilinged structure.

As Allegra stared at it, another image flickered in her mind. A tall man staring in fascination at an object standing within the small temple.

Allegra blinked, and a piece fell into place.

Atlantis.

Had Langcourt somehow discovered, or perhaps obtained Goran's stolen amphora? But why would Langcourt have gone through so much trouble to build a replica of the layout of Atlantis, to place the temple at its very center?

"Atlantis?" she asked softly, barely aware that she'd spoken.

"How do you know of it?" he asked, his tone harsh, accusing.

"I believe the answer would be that I saw it in a vision," Allegra replied, her face neutral.

"What vision? What did you see?"

Allegra shrugged. "I am not entirely sure what it meant. I recall seeing this place. And I saw the man who found it." Allegra took a step around the temple structure, and her view of the center was no longer obstructed by the column.

And her heart stilled.

In the center of the round domed temple structure sat a bronze amphora.

"Dear merciful Apollo," Allegra said on a gasp as she stared at the vessel. Allegra turned from the amphora to focus her fury on Langcourt. "Where did you get that? Is this what you do? Steal your way through the centuries?"

Even as she said the words, Allegra's heart thudded faster and faster.

Langcourt was immortal. The amphora was found in Atlantis. Goran had turned into an imbecilic wife-beater obsessed with this very vessel.

Goran had retained an unusually youthful countenance, which had troubled Lydia so greatly.

Allegra turned to face Langourt. "Which one are you?"

Langcourt flinched. "What? What do you mean?"

"Which of Goran's sons are you?" Allegra asked, the names flashing in her mind. She began to recite them, "Claudius, Severianus, Aquilinus, Iulius."

Allegra's eyes widened. How had she not seen it before? It had been staring her in the face the entire time.

"You're Lydia's son?" she whispered, the heat of tears burning her eyes.

Langcourt flinched, taking a sharp step away from her. "Do not utter that name in my presence. She is dead to me."

"Did you even know her to say such a thing?"

"My father told us enough."

"Goran fed you stories to steer you away from her wisdom. He wanted to keep you under his control." Allegra paused, her eyes darting around the room. "What happened to him?"

Langcourt surged toward Allegra, his arm raised, finger pointing. "Your people, your murdering assassins killed my father and all my brothers. Did you really think there was no blood on your hands Pythia?" Lancourt's rage overflowed, spit flying from his mouth as he flung the accusations at her.

Allegra shook her head. "I don't know about any assassins other than you and your brothers. What you have done? To your own family?"

"Not my family. The Pythias are not my family."

Allegra stilled, hearing the rage in the man's voice. "Then who is your family? Your father is Goran? And your mother is Lydia?"

Langcourt smirked. "You know this already, so why repeat the question?"

"I wanted to clarify. Do you know who Lydia was?" When Langcourt sent her a condescending glare, Allegra continued, "Do you know *what* Lydia was?"

Langcourt rushed Allegra, but she was faster. Opening her hand at her back, she felt Xales place the hilt of her bejeweled dagger in her palm, and in a smooth move she drew it around and pressed the deadly sharp blade against this throat.

"Do you know what your mother was, Severianus? Apart from a woman abused both mentally and physically by a man who was supposed to be caring for her?"

Langcourt shook his head, his eyes reflecting his uncertainty more than the fear of being sliced to death.

"Lydia was the first ever Oracle of Delphi."

"No," whispered Langcourt. "That is not true. The oracles are the reason we are always dying, always having to replenish our powers."

Allegra let out a dry laugh.

Everything suddenly made perfect sense to her now. "No. They were not the reason. You and your brothers were the product of the union of a Pythia and a man so obsessed with immortality that he stole the Elixir of Immortality from Atlantis. He kept it for himself, drank it until it sent him mad. Mad enough to beat the living hell out of his wife. He turned his sons away from her for fear that they would one day discover what they did to receive true immortality from their sire. That the only way they could retain that long life was to spill the blood of a Pythia."

"No that is not true."

"I think you know it is. He told you that the oracles were the reason for your failing immortality. He never told you that your own mother was the first Pythia to be named. He never told you that he killed Lydia with his bare hands because she opposed his desire to keep the amphora for himself. He never told you that that every single pythia you killed were the daughters of your mother, every single one of those women you and your brothers have been killing for three thousand years were your sisters, your family."

Allegra found herself breathless at her monologue, and found a shocked Langcourt, staring from her face to the amphora.

"It's empty you know. He consumed it all, every last drop of the Elixir is gone."

"All he wanted was for us to live," Langcourt insisted. "And the Pythias sent their assassins after us, shadowing us everywhere we went."

"Is it any wonder that they tried to avenge the deaths of the Pythias? I don't know of any Pythian Assassins, but it seems to me after Lydia was murdered by your father, the priests and priestesses of Delphi already would have had a good sense of what Goran's intentions were. And if they didn't know when Lydia was killed, they would have known when Lucia was killed."

Langcourt shook his head. "No. Back then there were no Pythian Assassins. Claudinius was sent to kill Kassandra, but he failed and our father made a second attempt."

Allegra snorted, driving the blade into Langcourt's throat. "It's probably a good thing he failed. But then again, with his hands dirty with the blood of his wife, what difference would the blood of his daughter have been?"

Langcourt let out a low cry, and Allegra let go of him as he staggered and sucked in air, as though struggling to breathe.

A part of Allegra grieved for this man, who now lay on the floor broken, centuries of blood on his soul, bearing the responsibility of the decimation of his entire bloodline.

But Langcourt was shaking his head, denying the truth. He surged to his feet, propelling himself at her. And Allegra merely reacted.

She raised her dagger. And Langcourt slammed into it, the blade sinking hilt deep between his ribs, straight into his heart.

She let out a cry, her instinct warning her that this man, despite everything he'd done, was still family. Even though the visions of him killing Cathenna still haunted her dreams.

Langcourt sagged against Allegra, his weight resting full upon her body, forcing her to lower him to the floor, the dagger still embedded within his chest. He lay back, swallowing hard, struggling for breath. "They're all dead," he whispered. "We killed them all..." Tears pooled in his eyes and ran down the side of his face.

Allegra found it hard to feel sorry for him, but she forced herself to shake her head. "Not all."

He coughed, blood dribbling from the corner of his mouth. "You," he said, voice gurgling, "you lived."

"Not only me." Allegra shook her head, refusing to say more, but the sight of the surge of elation in his eyes was her undoing. She let out a soft sigh and as the light faded from his eyes she whispered the words in his ear, "Cathenna's daughters all lived. Our family will survive."

The words spoken, Allegra watched as Langcourt—no, Severianus—took his last breath.

The man who had dogged Allegra's steps and had been so intent on killing her was dead.

Her only living blood-relative that she had touched with her own hands was dead.

CHAPTER 42

"There she goes again, stealing all the glory," said a voice from behind Allegra.

Taking a deep breath, she turned to face Athena. A rueful smile spread on Allegra's face. "Sorry? It was a life-or-death situation."

Her words echoed around the strange cavern that Langcourt had built beneath his villa.

"We saw that. Looked more like a reunion to me," said Max, his eyes dark with sadness as he walked over to her. "I'm so sorry you had to be the one." He gathered Allegra up within his arms and held on tight, feeding his energy into her body.

Allegra hugged him back and then took a step away, a little awkward what with them being in the same room as Langcourt's corpse.

Xales appeared at Allegra's right-hand side, his expression solemn too.

Allegra glared at him, then bestowed the same expression upon Max and Athena. "You were all here? You ever heard of lending a hand? I was almost killed."

"No, you weren't," said Xales, chuckling. "You had it under control."

"Fine. You do not have to say it. I've heard it before."

Despite Allegra's words, Xales continued, "If you had really needed my help, I would have assisted."

Allegra glanced over at Max.

"For once, I agree with Xales," Max replied, trying and failing to quell his grin. "You were in control the entire time."

Then, Athena stepped close and threw a hand around Allegra's shoulders. "I'm with those guys," she said as she began to guide Allegra out of the Atlantis replica room.

Allegra glanced over her shoulder at Max who hurried to catch up. "Lusitania?"

"Neptune found the device in the old chasm from the last quake. It was boarded up a century ago with lead-lined sheets which messed with his ability to hear."

"And the added advantage of that was the lead suppressed the signal so the bomb wouldn't have gone off even if Neptune hadn't gotten to it in time," Athena said, smiling brightly.

Allegra sighed. Though filled with sadness for Langcourt's terrible life and tragic end, Allegra felt the love of the people who surrounded her.

She was looking forward to returning home to the Charrúa estate, to writing everything down in the Codex Pythia Allegra. So many things had fallen into place at the same moment that her head was still spinning. But, even though it was all over, there were still a few things that needed to be recorded, if only for the next Pythia's education. There was still the matter of Jocasta and what could possibly be done to help her mother in the future. And as Allegra had told Langcourt, the family had survived. Cathenna's daughters were somewhere.

Whether they were alive was something Allegra needed to know, and she planned to do whatever she could to find out. But, in the meantime, all she wanted to do was to go home.

She let out a soft laugh. "I believe our work here is done"

Max leaned over and kissed her on the forehead. "Until next time."

Allegra grinned as she replied, "Until next time."

~ THE END ~
Allegra's adventures continue in
Dark Prophecy

ACKNOWLEDGMENTS

A special thanks to my JIT readers who helped make Shadow Sight even better: Teresa S, Bryan Ellis, Julie Pederick, and Pat Raab. And thank you to the rest of the JIT and ARC readers who took the time to read and review Shadow Sight. Thank you for all of your support!

FREE STARTER LIBRARY - JOIN MY NEWSLETTER

Get the following titles FREE when you subscribe to my newsletter.

Tee's Newsletter

http://smarturl.it/TeesMailingList

ABOUT THE AUTHOR

I have been a writer from the time I was old enough to recognize that reading was a doorway into my imagination. Poetry was my first foray into the art of the written word. Books were my best friends, my escape, my haven. I am essentially a recluse but this part of my personality is impossible to practice given I have two teenage daughters, who are actually my friends, my tea-makers, my confidantes… I am blessed with a husband who has left me for golf. It's a fair trade as I have left him for writing. We are both passionate supporters of each other's loves – it works wonderfully…

My heart is currently broken in two. One half resides in South Africa where my old roots still remain, and my heart still longs for the endless beaches and the smell of moist soil after a summer downpour. My love for Ma Afrika will never fade. The other half of me has been transplanted to the Land of the Long White Cloud. The land of the Taniwha, beautiful Maraes, and volcanoes. The land of green, pure beauty that truly inspires. And because I am so torn between these two lands – I shall forever remain cross-eyed.

Stalk Tee here:
www.tgayer.com
tee@tgayer.com

f facebook.com/TGAyerAuthor

🐦 twitter.com/TGAyerAuthor

BB bookbub.com/profile/t-g-ayer